"He's threatened to blow up the station if you don't go on the eleven o'clock news," Chandler said.

"He also said he'd kill another one of your patients," he added.

"I'll do it," Molly said, ignoring Chandler's harsh, disapproving look. "He could kill another innocent person. I don't want that to happen."

"There has to be a better option. Molly, I don't like this." He reached out and allowed his fingertip to trace the line of her jaw. The look in his eyes increased her pulse tenfold. "I've got a bad feeling about this," he murmured.

Molly reached up and covered his hand with hers. "This—the broadcast? Or this—me?"

Tilting his head slightly to the right, Molly's breath caught as his head dipped toward hers. His mouth hovered above hers as he whispered, "I look at you and all I can think of is this...."

Dear Harlequin Intrigue Reader,

This July, Intrigue brings you six sizzling summer reads. They're the perfect beach accessory.

* We have three fantastic miniseries for you. *Film at Eleven* continues THE LANDRY BROTHERS by Kelsey Roberts. Gayle Wilson is back with the PHOENIX BROTHERHOOD in *Take No Prisoners*. And B.J. Daniels finishes up her McCALLS' MONTANA series with *Shotgun Surrender*.

* Susan Peterson brings you *Hard Evidence*, the final installment in our LIPSTICK LTD. promotion featuring stealthy sleuths. And, of course, we have a spine-tingling ECLIPSE title. This month's is Patricia Rosemoor's *Ghost Horse*.

* Don't miss Dana Marton's sexy stand-alone title, *The Sheik's Safety*. When an American soldier is caught behind enemy lines, she'll fake amnesia to guard her safety, but there's no stopping the sheik determined on winning her heart.

Enjoy our stellar lineup this month and every month!

Sincerely,

Denise O'Sullivan
Senior Editor
Harlequin Intrigue

FILM AT ELEVEN

KELSEY ROBERTS

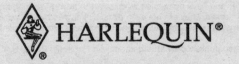

HARLEQUIN®

TORONTO • NEW YORK • LONDON
AMSTERDAM • PARIS • SYDNEY • HAMBURG
STOCKHOLM • ATHENS • TOKYO • MILAN • MADRID
PRAGUE • WARSAW • BUDAPEST • AUCKLAND

ISBN 0-373-88629-2

FILM AT ELEVEN

www.eHarlequin.com

Printed in U.S.A.

ABOUT THE AUTHOR

Kelsey Roberts has penned more than twenty novels, won numerous awards and nominations, and landed on bestseller lists, including *USA TODAY* and the Ingrams Top 50 List. She has been featured in the *New York Times* and the *Washington Post,* and makes frequent appearances on both radio and television. She is considered an expert in why women read and write crime fiction, as well as an excellent authority on plotting and structuring the novel.

She resides in south Florida with her family.

CAST OF CHARACTERS

Chandler Landry—Popular news anchor, and hometown hero, too good-looking for his own good. His complacent life becomes complicated and challenging when he meets Molly Jameson, then finds himself *becoming* the story on the eleven o'clock news, instead of reporting it.

Molly Jameson, M.D.—A psychiatrist with issues of her own. Her quiet, carefully controlled life becomes a media circus when she meets the fascinating Chandler Landry, and a murderer pulls her into his deranged and deadly game.

Peter Geller—A fanatic with a mission… Could it be murder?

Gavin Templesman, M.D.—A respected professor of psychiatry. Molly's mentor and Chandler's friend. But could he also be a killer?

Verna Geller—She's lost her head worrying over her son, but at this stage in her life there's nothing she can do to help him.

L. S. Wyatt—Molly's favorite author. But does he have a killer secret?

Chapter One

Molly Jameson considered ways to kill herself.

Figuratively at least.

She wasn't shy so much as intensely private, which made her current situation disconcerting.

She was vain enough to wonder for the umpteenth time if her clothing was right. Hopefully, the dark-navy suit would convey professionalism to the audience. She'd pinned her long blond hair into a loose twist, but several strands had fallen free. Her stomach flip-flopped yet again as she tried to smooth them back into place.

"Five minutes, Dr. Jameson," a masculine-looking woman in jeans and a T-shirt said as she adjusted the microphone attached to her bulky headset.

Molly nodded and smiled. Outwardly she hoped to appear cool and calm and tried not to think that she might be the very first person to throw up live on Montana's most popular morning news show.

Her eyes darted around the chaotic television studio. He leaned against the desk in the center of the large room. He had an easy, engaging smile and seemed completely comfortable.

And why wouldn't he? Chandler Landry *was* WMON-TV. His image was splashed on buses and billboards all over the place. Tilting her head, Molly studied him from the relative obscurity of her position behind one of three large cameras positioned around the set.

It wasn't any secret that Chandler Landry was considered one of the most eligible bachelors in the greater Helena-Jasper area. He had it all—looks, breeding, money, class and confidence.

Molly gave him serious bonus points in the looks department. He was more than six feet of sculpted muscle and genetic perfection wrapped in a perfectly tailored designer suit. His skin was deeply tanned but not leathery. His eyes were light brown, rimmed in dark, inky lashes. The only flaw—if she could call it that—was a slightly crooked smile. But it wasn't really a flaw. Nope, it was endearing and completely nonthreatening. On any other man, it would have been a sneer. But on Chandler it added an innocent allure that gave him that air of boyish charm.

"We're coming out of commercial," headset woman said, motioning Molly toward the brightly lit set. "Follow me."

Molly did, feeling all of her insecurities knot in

the pit of her belly. Silently she cursed Gavin Templesman. Only her beloved mentor could have conned her into doing this silly segment. Gavin knew how she felt about being in the public eye. He also knew how badly she wanted her book to succeed. She wanted to help people. That didn't mean she wanted to sit under a circle of hot lights and have the intrusive camera trained on her face for the next ten minutes. She knew her stuff. Saying something inappropriate or becoming tongue-tied wasn't going to be a problem for her. No matter how much she disliked the artifice of the television studio.

No, what she didn't enjoy was the feeling of vulnerability and discomfort she felt as Chandler Landry strolled across the set toward her. She folded her hands loosely in her lap as she watched him approach, willing her erratic heartbeat to slow and her breathing to remain even. Hard to imagine, but he was even better looking in person than on her twenty-seven-inch screen at home.

She hoped he wasn't a shaking-hands kinda guy. Her palms were slightly damp. Which annoyed her no end.

"Dr. Jameson," Chandler greeted with a smile that she felt all the way to her toes.

She subtly brushed her right hand on her skirt before taking the hand he offered and struggled to keep her knees from buckling. Up close, Chandler was a devastating sight to behold. The faint scent of his cologne was as intriguing as the fact that his palm was slightly callused. Why would a pretty boy have calluses?

"Mr. Landry," she greeted, forcing a lightness to her tone. "I feel like I know you already."

"Most people do," he replied easily. "The price you pay for being invited into the homes of viewers day in and day out."

"We all have our crosses to bear," she countered, dropping his hand.

"We're back in fifteen," a voice thundered through the studio.

Chandler held out a chair for her, presenting Molly with what she assumed was her first in a series of humiliations. In spite of her heels, she was forced to climb up on to the stool, and her perfectly professional navy pumps fell about an inch shy of the foot bar.

"Ten seconds, Chandler."

He rolled her into place. "Sit on the back of your jacket," Chandler suggested. "It looks better on camera."

"I thought I was here to give advice to your callers," she said as she adjusted the bunched lapels of her suit.

He clipped a microphone to the creamy silk tie that complemented his gunmetal-gray shirt. "This is television, sweetheart. Ninety percent of it is how you look."

"How positively shallow," she muttered as she scooted the hem of her jacket beneath her hips. *Sweetheart?* What a condescending ass.

"People don't tune in for ugly."

"In five," the bodyless voice announced.

"Lucky for you."

Chandler tossed her an easy smile. "Thanks, I think."

"In four."

Molly felt like a few thousand nerve endings wired for sound. While the studio was relatively quiet, everyone was watching the two of them. She felt like a zoo exhibit, and had to force herself not to fiddle with her hair and clothes. Something she rarely did. She was uncomfortably self-conscious and hoped to God it didn't show. She took a deep calming breath and let it out slowly.

Better.

"Three."

Her breathing was fine. It was her heart rate that was the problem. Nerves, anticipation and, damn it, the close proximity of Chandler Landry had her hyperaware. *How did I allow myself to get talked into this?*

"Two."

Chandler patted her hand just as one of the large cameras wheeled closer to them. "Good luck, Doc."

Headset woman brought her hand down and

pointed at Chandler just as a large red light came on above the teleprompter attached to the camera lens.

"Good morning, again, Montana. I'm here in the studio this morning with author and psychiatrist Martha Jameson."

Molly felt a trickle of perspiration dribble down between her shoulder blades. Part of it was the bright lights but most of it was palpable, intense fear.

"Dr. Jameson's latest book," Chandler continued, holding her book up as he spoke. "*The Relationship Mambo,* has just been released by University Press. Good morning, Dr. Jameson."

"Good morning," she replied in a hideously scratched voice.

"I was reading your book last night and I was struck by the fact that you advocate casual physical encounters in this day and age."

Leave it to a man to focus on the sex parts. Out of context, of course. This was going to be the longest ten minutes of her life. "Actually," she began, treading the waters between being pissed and terrified. "You've misstated my position." She ignored the dark flash in his eyes. "Sexuality is part of human nature. And while the ideal situation would be physical intimacy as part of a meaningful, committed relationship, that isn't always practical. The chapter you referred to is a discussion of the double standard that exists in our society. I was simply stating my opinion that women should take ownership over their sexuality just as men have done since the dawn of time."

"That's great in theory, but doesn't society frown on women being promiscuous?"

"I'm not advocating promiscuity, Mr. Landry. I'm acknowledging that women have the same physical needs as men." And apparently the same homicidal tendencies, Molly thought, wanting to smack that smug smile off his handsome face. Strangely, her heartbeat felt just fine and dandy now.

Great looking—yes. But smug, arrogant and very sure he was the be all and end all for any woman he met.

Nice try, Molly thought, narrowing her eyes slightly, but no cigar. It would take a better man than you are, Gunga Din.

Chandler smiled and winked. "Let's hope every woman out there adopts your philosophy. Dr. Jameson will answer any of your relationship questions. Call the number at the bottom of your screen." Chandler flipped her book open to a premarked page. He glanced down, then looked at her from under his brows as if surprised. "You also advocate divorce, Dr. Jameson."

Molly's blood boiled as she tried to maintain her fake smile. "Again you've misinterpreted my position." *Read for comprehension, pretty boy!* "I advocate divorce in situations where there is abuse, both physical and emotional."

"Or lack of love," he read.

"Which is a form of emotional abuse, Mr. Landry. Relationships are living things. They need fuel to survive. If there is no love, the relationship withers and dies." *Which is exactly what I'd like to have happen to you!*

"You don't confine your advice to men and women," he continued. "You write extensively about parent-child relationships, as well. Do you have children, Dr. Jameson?"

"No. My book is based on research and almost a decade as a therapist."

"Isn't it hard for you to hold yourself out as an authority on children when you've never had any of your own?"

"Psychiatrists often can't have firsthand knowledge of a given situation. For example, a doctor doesn't have to beat his wife in order to understand the dynamic of spousal abuse."

He gave her a slight nod of recognition. "We've got John on line one. Go ahead, John."

"Yes," a deep voice crackled through the studio. "My life sucks."

"This is morning television, John," Chandler warned politely. "Watch the language."

"Anyway," John's voice sounded annoyed and

tense. "I've got a crappy job. My mother's always ragging me. The government screwed me."

"Doctor?" Chandler interrupted. He gave Molly a "help me" look.

"John, it sounds to me like you're overwhelmed right now. I suggest you take some 'me' time."

"I can't. I need my lousy job to pay my bills. And my mother needs me. I do everything for her."

Molly heard the anger and torment in the voice. "You have to make a choice, John. I hear your frustration. When we're in that place, it affects everything we do. You have to take responsibility for your own happiness. If your job is making you miserable, then find another job. As for your mother, give yourself permission to take a break."

"She needs me."

"That may well be. But you need you, too. Once you're happy and fulfilled, you'll find that the other pieces of your life fall into place. Find something that will make you happy, John. One thing. Then do it."

"We've got to take the next caller, John, good luck," Chandler said, pressing one of the blinking lights on the phone in front of him. He greeted the caller by name as provided by his producer.

Chandler smiled over at the small woman with the authoritative tone. She was too damned cute to be such a tight ass. He'd actually found her book enlightening, insightful even. His producer had insisted he mention the section on sex. The plan had been to mention it once to please the higher-ups, and then move on. Then he saw Molly Jameson.

She was a prim, professional package at serious odds with the frank discussion on sexuality he'd read. This, of course, was far, far sexier. There was something incredibly appealing about this woman. He guessed she was much more than a pretty face hidden beneath a layer of navy linen.

Chandler had to struggle to look interested as the next few callers chimed in. Three women involved with losers who couldn't or wouldn't stop the cycle of the dead-end relationship. To her credit, Molly seemed to be taking it all in stride.

"…time for you to put a period on this relationship and move on," Molly advised. "Don't look at it as a failure, think of the two years you spent with Tony as a learning experience."

"Thank you."

Chandler listened as his producer's voice boomed in his ear, then said, "Dr. Jameson, our first caller, John, is calling back."

"Hello again, John," she said.

Chandler watched as she wiped her damp palms across her lap. Odd that such a confident woman should be so uncomfortable on camera.

"I took your advice," the caller stated.

"That's good, John," Molly replied, her eyes narrowed suspiciously.

"Hey, John?" Chandler asked, "You only called a few minutes ago. How did you change your life in such a short period of time?"

"I did what she said," John answered. "I just killed my mother."

Chapter Two

"It worked! They bought it." Feeling triumphant and high on success, he looked at his companion.

Approval. Admiration. Reading that in those eyes eased the rapid pounding of his heart. He felt fortified, bolstered. Because he'd done his part perfectly, the plan was in motion.

"Patience, son."

Oh, for— He didn't *want* to be patient. Not anymore. Patient sucked. It was his time, damn it! *His* turn. Without responding to the unnecessary caution, he rose and went into the tiny, galley-style kitchen and ran water over his hands until the stream went from red, to pink, to clear. Grabbing the vegetable brush his mother kept in a frog on the lip of the sink, he began scrubbing at his finger tips. Who knew it would be so hard to get blood out from under his nails?

How like his mother to be a pain in the ass even in death.

His companion stood, collected his briefcase and

brought it over to the kitchen table. The metal locks clicked loudly as he depressed the tabs. "This should tide you over through the next phase."

Drying his hands, he moved to ogle the tidy rows of money displayed neatly in the open leather brief-case. Wiping his palms down the leg of his pants first, he lifted one banded stack of bills. Heavier than he'd've thought. His heartbeat sped up as he fanned the crisp notes, enjoying the breeze created against his face. "This is great."

His companion pulled the money from his grip and dropped it back into the case with an authoritative *plop*. He closed the lid and snapped the locks back in place. As if *he* had the right. As if *he* still owned the money. "This is to be used as we agreed."

"I know." Of course he knew. Hadn't he gone over and over this countless times? He wasn't a moron. Still, as much as he resented it, he craved the man's approval.

"You must stay focused. Too much is at stake here." His expression softened as he returned the cash. Next, he reached beneath the bills and took out a metal rod with a circular emblem welded to one end. "You know what to do?"

Once again he felt torn; irritated by the implication that he didn't know what he was doing, and then annoyed by his need for approval. He nodded stiffly. "I rigged the propane tank out back." Why did he always have to explain himself? Hadn't he proven that he was loyal and capable? The right choice to lead them toward their destiny? Hadn't he made the ultimate sacrifice?

"Can I trust you to handle the rest of the arrangements on your own?"

"Of course," he answered, resentment building at *always* having his abilities questioned. "I've got it under control."

His companion nodded, turned to leave, then hesitated. "There is much at stake."

Yeah, yeah, yeah. "I know that." Feeling more in control, now that he had the money and he'd accomplished the biggest hurdle, he reined in his temper. This powerful man would see a display of temper as a sign of weakness. *Just you wait,* he thought, feeling smug and self-satisfied as he stood, shoulders slightly hunched, eyes downcast. *Just you freaking wait.* Soon *he'd* be the one making all the decisions. He'd be the big man in charge.

That was the goal.

That was his destiny.

He was so close to making his goal a reality.

"SPEAKING FROM EXPERIENCE, I don't agree."

"It was a *prank,* Dr. Jameson," Chandler insisted. "Do you have any idea how many times this sort of thing has happened in the past?"

Molly squared her shoulders, feeling mildly annoyed that she had to tilt her head back in order to hold his gaze. He was the *most* annoying man. And the prime reason she felt that way, she had to admit, was her body's visceral reaction to him. His insistence that the man on the phone had been pulling a prank was, in her professional judgment, a huge mistake. The caller had sounded not only completely sincere, he'd sounded triumphant.

The fact that she was both annoyed *and* strangely attracted to Landry bugged the hell out of her. There weren't two more diametrically opposed people on the planet. "You have people committing and confessing to murders on air often, do you?" Molly demanded, trying to drag her libido back in line. Plenty of men had sparkling brown eyes and long dimples in their lean cheeks. Landry looked as though he had a delicious secret.

Molly didn't care to find out what that might be.

He was good-looking. So what? Jasper had hundreds of good-looking men.

He rolled those chocolate-colored eyes at her pithy comment, and made a dismissive sound that made her want to smack his smugly handsome face. A reaction that horrified her. Not only didn't she have a temper—under normal circumstances—but her training had taught her the pitfalls of physical violence. In under an hour this man had turned her into someone she didn't recognize.

She took a deep, calming breath and reminded herself that Chandler was a news reader, hardly in a position to assess the seriousness of a mentally disturbed person appropriately. "He—"

Chandler cut her off. "People seek attention, Molly. It's a risk and a reality on live TV. It was probably just some fool getting his kicks at our expense."

"I didn't get that sense," she replied, keeping her voice reasonable with an effort.

"We've got to clear the studio," Chandler gathered his script sheets into a pile and stood. "Let's go back to my office. We can wait for Seth there. I'm sure it was a joke," he assured her for the umpteenth time. Her gray-green eyes narrowed as she looked up at him, and he saw she wasn't going for his theory one bit. He sighed inwardly. She was a shrink. Hell, she'd see mental defect in everyone as a matter of course. "Sick," he said firmly, "but a joke nevertheless."

Clearly not convinced, Molly frowned slightly as she rose. Chandler didn't move back as she straightened, so they were closer together than two strangers would feel comfortable with. Her perfume drifted up to him. Something soft and subtle. Roses, he thought. Maybe with a touch of citrus. He stayed where he was, waited to see what Molly would do.

She held her ground. She might not be willing to show that his size and nearness intimidated her, but he sure as hell noticed the sudden increase of her pulse in the creamy hollow of her throat. Points to the lady.

"Maybe," she said, meeting his eyes unflinchingly. "But he sounded serious to me. I guess that's the problem with call-in therapy. It's really hard to diagnose someone as a sociopath over the phone."

He grinned, nice to meet a shrink with a sense of humor. Normally he found members of her profession way too serious, and frequently screwier than the people they purported to treat. For example their regular guest for the mental health segment Gavin Templesman. Now there was a guy filled with his own self-importance. Knowledgeable but pedantic and superior. Chandler thought the guy was an ass. He figured he should keep that opinion to himself, since he wasn't clear on the relationship between Templesman and Molly.

The lights in the studio dimmed. A broad hint from the control room.

"Are we going somewhere?" Molly asked pointedly. "Or are we staying here in the dark?"

He wouldn't mind standing in the dark with Dr. Molly a while longer, but Chandler figured she'd get a little cranky if he didn't move it.

"My office. He placed his palm against the small of her back to guide her out of the studio and toward his office. The stiffening of her spine was infinitesimal beneath his palm, but she didn't make a verbal protest. "You must know Dr. Templesman pretty well for him to suggest you fill in for him at the last minute."

She slanted him a look. "Was that a question?"

Yeah. He wanted to know if the old guy was her lover. Chandler smiled. "Are you partners or something?" Mentally, he added, *professional or otherwise?*

She blandly replied, "I've known him for twelve years," walking a little bit faster so that his hand fell away from her waist in a silent rebuke. Another point to the lady.

And a nice nonanswer, he thought. Her movement caused some of the silken strands of wheat-blond hair to slip from their neat bundle. His fingers itched to reach out and give a gentle tug, just enough so that her hair spilled over her shoulders. Instead, he shoved one hand into his pocket and dropped the other to his side. Best to keep his hands to himself…at least for now.

He paused at the entrance to his office and ushered her inside with a wave of his hand. "Make yourself comfortable," he suggested, grabbing two three-quarter-inch tapes off the chair. He put the tapes and his script into the top drawer of his desk. "Seth should be here shortly. Just a formality. While I'm sure the guy wasn't serious, the station will want to be sure to cover its ass. Just in case." Everyone was sue happy these days.

The base of his chair squeaked as he dropped into the battered leather cushions that conformed perfectly to his body. His eyes scanned Dr. Molly's very serious face. She was really pretty—wholesomely pretty, femininely pretty. And pretty much not interested in him, apparently.

This, of course, made Chandler that much more fascinated. Without vanity, he knew he was attractive and attractive to women. It had been a while since his advances, subtle as they were, had been coolly and politely rebuffed.

"You're staring," she commented. Her voice was soft, nonthreatening, almost observational. Despite the scrutiny, she neither shifted in her seat nor fidgeted under his perusal. More points to the lady. She was racking them up.

It irritated him a little that he couldn't get a read on her. Observing people was his forte. He flashed her his best and most effective smile. "You're a beautiful woman. It's my job to stare at you. Part of the Man Code."

No grin, no smile, not even a faint twinkle in her eyes. Flattery didn't impress her. Okay, he'd try another tack.

"Your book really was quite good."

Full-on, perfect-teeth smile. Okay, I get it. The way to this woman's heart was through her intellect.

"Thanks." A little of the frost left her eyes. "I'm surprised you read it. I'd expect someone like you to glance at the Table of Contents, maybe check out at a few chapter headings."

Chandler leaned back in his seat, stretching his

legs off to the side and crossing them at the ankles. She was really something. What, he wasn't yet sure. But her quick assessment of him stung. He shot her a cool look. "Someone like me?"

Her cheeks held just a hint of color. "I didn't mean to offend you."

That wasn't an apology, he surmised easily. Not a real one. She wasn't sorry she'd implied that he was too stupid to read, only that telling him as much wasn't supposed to be offensive.

"I like to read," he replied easily. "I'm especially fond of books with lots of colorful pictures."

Her cheekbones flamed. "I…I." She snapped her mouth shut as her brain scrambled for a way out. But there wasn't one. Taking a deep breath, she met his dark eyes and admitted, "You're right. That was an unkind way to put it. But the truth is, you've got a reputation as someone who, well, who…who…"

"Isn't too bright?"

She felt herself cringe. "Well, people don't usually mention your IQ, Mr. Landry. Any time you make the papers, there's usually mention of the fact that you're gorgeous and single. Montana's Second Most Eligible Bachelor, as I recall?"

"Imagine how pissed off I was at not being named number one," he countered. "And yes, I'm aware of the focus often placed on my appearance, but then, I work in a visual medium, so I can't really complain."

"I suppose not," Molly agreed. "I shouldn't have accepted the stereotype so easily. I do apologize." And boy, did she hate doing it too. *Stupid, stupid, stupid,* she told herself. Making a thoughtless comment like that to a man like this, was tantamount to poking a sharp stick through the bars of a lion's cage just to hear him roar. She knew better.

Chandler simply shrugged. Well, it wasn't all that simple. Not when the fabric of his jacket pulled taut against broad, hard muscle. Molly swallowed and willed her brain not to dwell on his physical attributes.

"Most of the time my, er, celebrity is a bonus. I can get into most of the decent restaurants without a prior reservation and I can usually find a date on short notice."

Molly mentally rolled her eyes but kept her gaze steady and her hands neatly in her lap. "Two important life skills," she told him dryly.

"That was pretty snippy," he said without even a hint of annoyance. "How about I get us some coffee?"

"That would be great," she agreed readily. Maybe a shot of caffeine would improve her mood.

Chandler rose from behind his desk, a large, powerful, charming male in his prime. Her mouth went dry. She inspected a slight hangnail on her thumb as he walked past her chair and disappeared. Leaving her free to explore his small, tidy office. She took a couple of quick, necessary breaths to control her heart rate. The man was potent.

She glanced around his office. The first thing that struck her was the organization. It wasn't just orderly; it was Obsessive-Compulsive-Disorder neat. His functional desk was gray laminate and formed an "L" shape out from the wall. He'd divided it into two separate and distinct areas. The portion facing the door was devoid of anything but the telephone. Not a pencil, not a scrap of paper, nothing. Just the telephone. With a perfectly coiled cord. Very precise.

On the short portion of the "L" sat a state-of-the-art laptop. It was one of the sleek, chrome models that supposedly traveled well. Next to the computer was a small tower of disks, color-separated and labeled in bold, block letters that were so perfectly matched in shape and size that she had to look twice to confirm they were handwritten.

Dropping her purse next to the chair, Molly rose and went to the first of three bookcases that lined the opposite wall. Black plastic videotape cases were lined like soldiers on the first three shelves. A closer inspection revealed that they were in alphabetical order. Seriously anal.

The second case was a collection of reference books, alphabetized and separated by size, color and topic. He had everything ranging from the *Annotated Laws of the State of Montana* to a *Zoologists Guide to Bears.* Pathologically anal.

Had it not been for the contents of the third book-case, she would have started wondering about his mental health. On these shelves she found glimpses of him as a man. There were several framed photographs. Many, she guessed, were family pictures. They seemed to cover decades. One in particular caught her eye. Carefully, she lifted it off the shelf. Nine sets of smiling eyes looked back at her.

She shivered at the mere thought of such a huge family. The parents made a handsome couple. Chandler obviously came by his good looks honestly. His father was a very handsome man and his mother was stunning. She looked quite out of place among all that testosterone.

She also looked sad, Molly thought. There was something in her clear-blue eyes that seemed distant, unconnected. Molly felt herself smile, the poor woman was probably sleep deprived. She probably hadn't had a decent night's sleep since the birth of her first of seven sons.

"I'm the cute one—second from the left," a slightly familiar male voice said from the doorway.

Molly turned to find Seth Landry smiling a greeting. He looked quite official in his sheriff's uniform. And her brain made the predictable comparisons. Seth, like Chandler, was tall, dark and incredibly fit. His smile was warm and charming. Charm seemed to be an inherited trait among the Landrys.

Molly replaced the picture in its spot and extended her hand as she stepped forward. "Nice to see you again, Sheriff."

"That's right," he acknowledged with a slight nod. "You worked with my nephew a few years back."

"How is Kevin?"

"Great. Spoiled. Adjusting to being a big brother."

"I ran into Callie at the grocery store," Molly recalled. "She had little Sheldon with her. He's adorable."

"I think so, but then, I'm the favorite uncle, so I'm prejudiced."

"I'm the favorite uncle," Chandler insisted. He moved past Seth to place two mugs of coffee onto the desk, then hugged Seth and gave him a loud slap on the back.

Molly looked on with a twinge of envy. It must be nice to have a sibling. She hadn't had that kind of physical contact with anyone since her father's death. While she adored Gavin, it wasn't the same. It wasn't this.

"Sorry to drag you out here," Chandler said. "I'm sure it's a waste of your time."

"I disagree," Molly insisted. "I think that once you review the call, Sheriff, you'll believe, like I do, that there is cause to investigate."

"I'll defer to you, Doctor," Seth replied easily. "Chandler rarely takes anything seriously enough. It's been a problem his entire life."

Chandler tossed his brother a "kiss-off" look, then turned his attention back to Molly.

Her pretty eyes were little more than angry gray-green slits. Her pale skin was flushed but otherwise perfect. She was beautiful. And she was wrong.

"I'm sure it was just a crank call," he reiterated.

"I disagree," she countered. "I think if you listen to the tape—I assume one was recorded?"

"Yes," Chandler supplied.

"It's being cued in the control room as we speak," Seth added. "I'd like the two of you to walk me through it."

"My pleasure," Molly said, spinning on her heel and walking ahead of them.

Chandler shook his head at the sight of her rigid back. His expression softened as his eyes dropped lower. Down to the gentle slope of her hips, lower still, to her shapely, toned legs. The woman had a great body.

Chandler's brother grabbed his upper arm, holding him back and leaning closer before whispering, "Killer body."

"You're an old married guy, you shouldn't be noticing bodies anymore. Killer or otherwise."

"Just doing my job," Seth retorted.

"How is admiring the good doctor's tush part of your job description?"

"Investigation." Seth shoved his Stetson back

against his forehead and tilted his head slightly to the right as they slowly followed Molly down the hallway.

"Knock it off," Chandler groused. "You have a beautiful wife. Go look at her."

"I do," Seth said on a contented sigh. "Every chance I get."

"Then leave this one for me." He saw Seth's reproachful look out of the corner of his eye. "What?"

"She knows Callie. And Sam. And Kevin. And Taylor."

Chandler's brain flashed the images of his sister-in-law, his brother Sam, their son, and the Landrys' housekeeper, Taylor Reese. None of the pictures in his mind deterred him from admiring the enticing view of Molly in her fitted navy suit. "So?"

Seth made a sound somewhere between a grunt and a groan. "Don't be stupid, Chandler. You know better than to fool around with a friend of the family. When it ends—and we both know it always does—there'll be divided loyalties and hell to pay."

Chandler shrugged, knowing there was some merit to Seth's argument. Very few things in life were as scary as the wrath of a woman. One surefire way to incur said wrath was to date and dump a friend. Women were amazing. Their friendships created a universal agreement that made the Musketeers look like pikers. Dump one and the others made you pay. Big-time.

"I'm just window-shopping," Chandler said. "No harm in that, is there?"

"With you?" Seth asked. "Hell yes. You're never satisfied by looking. Never were, never will be."

Chandler jabbed his brother in the ribs with his elbow. "I'll have you know I'm the picture of self-control."

Rolling his eyes, Seth snickered. "You're like a two-year-old, little brother. You need instant gratification. You see something you like, you want it five minutes ago. And you bore easily."

Chandler watched as Molly shifted her purse from one dainty hand to the other. "How could anyone get bored with such a stunning creature?"

"You'd find a way," Seth insisted. "Try some restraint. It builds character."

"Screw character," Chandler whispered as he donned his best poker face.

They reached the end of the corridor and Molly appeared to be at a loss. Placing his hand at the back of her waist, Chandler nudged her gently in the direction of the control booth. Inwardly he smiled as he felt her body shudder beneath his touch. To a lesser man, that might have been a deterrent. But he knew better. That small flinch was an acknowledgment, tangible proof that she was aware of his fingers splayed against her spine.

"In here," he said, stepping to the side of the door and gallantly making a production out of allowing her to enter first.

Seth stepped forward and mumbled, "Suck up."

"Jealous."

"Hardly. I've got a wife, remember?"

"Who wants a wife when you can have her?"

"Who says you can have her?" Seth countered. "She seems pretty uninterested to me."

"She won't be for long."

"Don't go there, Chandler. She's a nice lady. Been good to our family."

"And those are two very good reasons for me to invite her to dinner."

"Suit yourself," Seth sighed. "But when you mess this up, I won't save you from Callie or Taylor."

"Who says I'm going to screw up?"

"Your entire life history."

He shrugged and muttered, "I wish I'd been an only child." Still, Seth's words struck an unpleasant chord. Though he'd bite off his tongue before admitting it to his brother, Chandler knew his dating credentials fell far short of stellar. He did tend to rush into relationships, only to discover after the fact that he'd chosen poorly. But that didn't make him incapable of having a real relationship. Did it? He sighed. Okay, so he'd done some borderline wrong things. But never once, not even for a split second, had he ever intended to hurt anyone.

Molly was fascinated by the vastly complicated electronic equipment crammed into a small, two-tiered room. One entire wall was monitors. Some were tuned to network programming, others were blank, still others were live feeds from the cameras located in the studios.

There were two long consoles in the room, with too many switches, dials and colored buttons to count. Several casually attired people with headsets manned the control boards. Yanking off his headset, a rotund man in a rumpled golf shirt stepped forward to welcome them.

She recognized the voice immediately. He was the producer who had called her with arrangements to do *Good Morning Montana*. He was also the disembodied voice she'd heard over the studio's speakers.

"I'm Mike Murray," he said, offering a beefy hand, and looking at Seth over her shoulder. "We've got the tape all set-up, sheriff."

"Thank you," Seth said. "Mind if we do this in private?"

The producer looked perplexed. "Yeah, I do. This is a newsroom. If it turns out there's something to this call, then we have a responsibility to our viewers to stay on top of it."

Seth did not appear pleased. "You also have a responsibility not to hinder my investigation."

The burly producer seemed to be mulling it over.

Chandler stepped up and said, "Don't sweat it, Mike, I'll run the tape machine and if anything of interest comes of this, I'm on it."

As soon as the other employees were dismissed, Molly and Seth were given seats at the console. Chandler opted to lean against the edge of the second row, his fingers within easy reach of the machine's controls.

They watched the tape twice in silence, then Seth began asking for their impressions at various parts. After almost three hours, Molly had memorized every syllable of John's call.

"He's young," she said when the tape ended. "Early twenties."

"Why do you say that?" Seth asked.

"He mentions the government screwing him. Teenagers don't really have much interaction with the government."

"But he could be older than twenties, right?" Seth asked.

"Assuming he isn't a crackpot," Chandler spoke up, "his vocabulary is more in keeping with a young adult."

Molly turned and gave him a smile. "Very good. And I agree. He used 'lousy' and 'crappy' which would be more appropriate for a twenty-year-old than a thirty-five year old. He also said his mother *needed* him. It indicates an inflated sense of self-importance."

"Aren't all men self-important?"

Molly again had to smile at Chandler's question. "Pretty much," she agreed, amused. "But in this case, he lumps his mother in with all his other problems. It shows minimal separation. I would guess this guy hasn't had a great deal of life experience apart from his nuclear family."

"This is good, I think—" Seth's thought was interrupted by the sound of his cell phone. Grabbing it from the clip on his belt, Seth flipped it open and placed it against his ear. "Yes?" There was a lengthy pause, then "Say that again. Got it. I'll be right there."

"Problem?"

Seth's brow wrinkled into a deep frown that reached the corners of his eyes. "Maybe. Just got a 911 call for a floater in Spawn Creek."

"A woman?" Molly asked, a sick feeling in the pit of her stomach. "Could it be John's mother?"

"Won't know for a while." Seth stood and put his notepad into the breast pocket of his uniform shirt. "I've got to go."

"I'll go with you," Chandler offered.

Seth shook his head. "No way. I don't want any press on this just yet."

"It's a crime scene, Seth," Chandler argued. "I've got every right to be there with a camera crew."

Molly saw a flash of anger pass between the two men. It was so intense that she actually flinched.

"No camera, Chandler. Not on this one."

"Why? What's so special about this one?"

"It's bad," Seth answered slowly. "Really bad."

Chapter Three

"Is she still hurling?" Seth asked without turning. He was crouched close to the remains, overseeing the horrific but necessary task of pulling the torso from the brackish shallows of Spawn Creek.

Chandler glanced over his shoulder to where he'd hurriedly parked the car. Molly was doubled over behind a shrub, about fifty discreet yards away. He didn't blame her one bit. It was everything he could do to keep his own revulsion in check. "Yep. We've all been there." He felt genuine sympathy for the woman but was a little perplexed by her reaction. "She has an M.D., you'd think she'd be better equipped for something like this."

Seth shot him a quick glance. "I don't think anyone can be prepared for something like this. *Hell*, I'm not prepared. What kind of animal could do this?"

Chandler shrugged, knowing his brother's question was rhetorical. There wasn't an explanation for this kind of savagery. At least, none that any sane person could conjure. This was brutal, ugly and violent. As bad as anything he'd seen during his tour in the first Gulf War.

"It's going to be tough to get an ID," Seth remarked to the crime-scene tech preparing to transport the remains. "Whoever did this went to a lot of trouble to make it virtually impossible for us to identify her."

"Unless you can find the rest of her," Chandler suggested. That thought made his stomach clench with renewed repugnance.

Seth stood and expelled an audible breath. Chandler knew his brother well. Seth would do whatever it took to find justice for this poor woman.

As the tech was lifting the remains onto the body bag, Chandler spotted something. "What's that?" he asked, pointing in the general direction of a dark impression on the torso's left shoulder.

Both men peered closer, examining the bizarre marking. "Maybe that'll help you with the identification." Chandler suggested.

"Looks postmortem," the crime tech offered as he stopped to photograph the marking from various angles. "A burn of some kind."

"It's something," Seth remarked, though his tone didn't indicate much hope that this bit of information would actually bear fruit. "I want the M.E. on this now," he instructed. "Don't want to wait for the full report. Have someone send over the photographs as soon as they're printed. And get me the estimate on time of death."

"That's going to be hard," the tech replied. "The water temperature is fifty-two degrees, hard to get exacts on floaters."

"I'll take approximates for now," Seth fairly barked, frustration evident in his tone. He turned to Chandler. "Why don't you take the doctor back to her car. I've got my guys coming out here for a full search of the banks and divers on their way to see if the rest of our Jane Doe might be somewhere upstream."

"Three different rivers and two lakes feed into this creek, bro. That's going to be like looking for a needle in a stack of needles."

Seth shrugged. "True, so after you drop off Dr. Jameson, give Savannah a call and let her know I probably won't be home for a while."

"Will do," Chandler agreed, placing a hand on his brother's shoulder to give a comforting squeeze. "God. Do you think—"

"This was the work of your morning caller?"

Seth met his gaze. "My gut tells me yes. Guy calls in, says he offed his mother? If it wasn't, this would stretch coincidence." Seth shot a sympathetic glance across the clearing. "I think that also means you owe the good doctor an apology."

"One of the first things on my list," Chandler agreed easily. Molly looked rather pathetic, and his protective instincts came rushing to the fore. It surprised him that he should feel such a strong desire to walk over and pull her into his arms. She was, after all, an acquaintance. *For now,* his brain suggested. So he lusted for her and he didn't like seeing her so upset. That didn't make him a creep. Actually, he thought, his posture straightening, it made him one hell of a nice guy. Hopefully she would notice. He gave Seth's shoulder a final squeeze. "Keep me in the loop on this one, okay?"

"You were the first point of contact for him. You're already in the loop." He jerked his chin across the field to Molly. "So's she."

"My thought exactly," Chandler said grimly. "Keep me posted?"

"Will do." Seth was back in sheriff mode as he strode to talk to his people. Chandler went the other way. Walking through the long grass, he was mindful of each step, knowing the police would be combing every inch of the area for evidence over the next several hours. *So what was the deal?* he wondered. What kind of sicko could hack a woman up like that, and, most disturbing, was it John? Was this the mother he had claimed to have killed? If so, something told him this was the beginning rather than the end.

He found Molly sitting in the grass. Her slender shoulders lifted and fell as she sucked in deep, calming breaths. She seemed to have regained most of her composure, even though her skin was still a pasty shade of gray.

He reached his hand out to pull her up. She wobbled unsteadily. He shot out his other hand to support her elbow, and at the same time she put a shaky hand on his chest to brace herself. "Ready to go?" he asked.

"About half an hour ago would've been fine. Thanks, I'm okay now." She took a small step back, and reluctantly he let go, allowing her to brush the grass and debris from the back of her skirt in what he recognized as a "hands off" sign. Interesting.

He pointed to his car. "How about I run you home?"

"Oh, I—"

He started walking toward the row of vehicles parked off to the side. "I've got a bottle of water in the car. You still look a little green." And, God only knew, he *felt* a little green himself.

She gave him a small smile. "Sorry about that."

"No need to apologize. I've seen battle-tested soldiers and seasoned detectives have the same reaction. It's basic human nature to be nauseated seeing something like that."

"I should have been able to handle it. I thought I'd graduated from being a total wuss."

Chandler smiled sympathetically. He gave her points for maintaining her sense of humor. "I had no idea there was a graduation process for wussiness."

She rolled her pretty, green eyes. "Silly, I know." Her soft mouth curved. "But medical schools insist on future doctors having some sort of qualifications before they practice. I made it. But unfortunately not before earning the nickname 'Meltdown Molly' after my first anatomy class. Saw the body on the slab and dropped like the proverbial stone."

He laughed. "Since you've got an M.D. after your name, I assume you overcame that tendency."

"Yeah. So did I," she said on a deep sigh. "Until a little while ago." Her eyes flickered toward the activity on the shore, then back to him. "That poor, poor woman. Only someone consumed with hatred could've done something that vicious."

"There are a lot of sick bastards out there," he agreed grimly. "I believe you nailed it this morning. Caller John wasn't a hoax."

She stopped in midstride to clutch his arm, surprising him by the strength of her grip. And his own reaction to having her slender fingers clasped around his bicep. Heat shot up his arm. Talk about bad timing.

"Is that—I mean is *she* John's mother?"

"Since Jasper isn't the murder capital of the world, it only makes sense that whoever called in this morning was telling the truth."

"Sick bastard is right," she agreed under her breath, surprising him again.

Her hand fell away and they continued up to

where his car waited. "Isn't that a little harsh for a shrink? Aren't you supposed to understand depraved behaviors?"

"Understand—sure. I also understand that anyone who can decapitate a woman's head, as well as her hands and feet, deserves whatever severe remedy is available from the courts. Hopefully something that involves a lethal injection after he's spent all those years of appeals locked in his cell watching an endless loop of videos of his victim."

HE WISHED HE'D MADE A VIDEO so he could watch himself killing her over and over again. But he wasn't that stupid. Hell, he didn't even have a video camera. He'd have to make do with the sharp, full-color mental images of the Big Event.

"This is so cool!"

He looked at his friend and easily accepted the praise. *Now if you could just see the movie in my head—that would really impress you.* "All I have left to do is connect these two wires."

He liked having an audience as he worked. Even if the audience was only two of his peers. Well, he didn't think they were his peers. While they were the same age and had grown up together, the other men were followers, and he was a leader. Soon everyone would know that. Soon everyone would see that he really was destined for greatness.

"Will this, like, totally blow up the whole street, or what?"

He finished capping the twisted wires and fit them inside the remote-control device. "It'll get the job done."

"So then we call the TV station and the papers and—"

His pointed stare silenced his friend. "*We* don't do anything. *I* make the decisions."

"We're in this, too," the youngest member of the group whined.

Man, he hated whining. It reminded him of *her.* And thinking about her always made his heart race and his palms sweat with helpless rage. *Ha!* he thought triumphantly. *Not so helpless now, am I Mama?* He gave the other man a cold look. "Do you want to end up like my mother?"

The younger man gulped and shook his shaved head.

"This operation has one leader and that's me." Jesus. Power was euphoric. His heart raced, but this time from excitement. It was all coming together. Just like he'd said it would. Like a ball rolling downhill, his confidence gained momentum. He was empowered by his own smarts and skill. "I chose you all," he looked from one to the other. The boss man. In charge. Master of his own fate. Hell, yeah!

"Handpicked each one of you," he said as if it were God's hand that had chosen them. And why not? He was the next best thing. "This mission is critical. If my orders aren't followed to the letter, or if either of you gets out of line, you'll be replaced." He paused for effect. Nice, real nice. They were about wetting their pants. "Is that clear?"

He gloated inside as they nodded, eyes wide, showing fear and demonstrating the respect he so richly deserved. His mentor was right. He was a natural-born leader. This was his destiny. It was so close now, he could almost taste it.

"We'll store the bomb in the shed out by the old Greeley Mine," he told them.

"Why not just plant it now?"

Again his authority was being challenged and again he felt a sudden and intense rush of rage. Pain, sharp and intense stabbed behind his eyes, and blood rushed to his skin like fiery sheet lightning. He grabbed his questioner, balled up his fist and punched him. The other man staggered backward from the blow, crashing into a table and scattering components onto the floor.

"Don't." He got a grip on the fallen man's shirt and hauled him to his feet.

"Ever." He punched him again, this time blood spurted from his friend's nose.

"Question." He pulled back and gut punched him. His pal doubled over.

"Me." He jerked up his knee and made contact with the other man's chin.

Bleeding and unconscious, the guy crumpled to the floor, then lay motionless.

Power. He had it. He was invincible now. He gave the other man a hard look. "Any more questions?"

"Not me, dude."

As it should be. "Good." Though his knuckles hurt from the contact with the man's jaw, that little bit of physical exertion had allowed him to release some of the fury surging through his system. Not as much as killing him would've done, but killing the weasel dog wasn't in the cards. He smiled inwardly. At least not today. He still had a use for his good old buddy.

His heartbeat resumed its normal cadence as his blood pressure went down. "There's still some covert work to be done." He wiped the spatter of his victim's blood from his hand to his jeans and stepped over the man's extended legs. "I'll be giving each of you a specific assignment. Are you ready for your instructions?"

MOLLY ARRIVED BACK at her modest apartment feeling utterly exhausted. On the plus side, her stomach had quieted. On the minus side, she was struggling to push the horrific image of the mutilated torso from her mind.

She parked and walked the short distance to her front door, inserted her key and breathed in the calming scent of familiarity. Since she lived alone, the scents from her abundance of potpourri and candles were the closest substitute she had to hearing "Welcome home, honey, how was your day?"

As was her habit, she dropped her purse and keys on the foyer table and automatically pressed the button on her telephone's answering machine. The first four messages were to her home number. Three hang-ups and one from her mentor Gavin Templesman.

"Molly, honey, I heard about the show and I'm just calling to see how you're dealing with it. Call me when you get in."

She'd call Gavin back later. When she no longer had a burning desire to damn him to hell for having her fill in on the show. Intellectually she knew that Gavin wasn't responsible for getting her dragged into the murder of that poor woman, emotionally she felt like sharing some of the bad karma.

Two beeps sounded, followed by a mechanical voice announcing, "Switching to remote message retrieval. Inbox for Dr. Jameson accessed."

She stripped off her jacket as she listened to the lone message. Her ten-o'clock appointment for the next morning was canceling. Again.

"Lester," she said as the message ended, "that's three appointments in a row, pal. I'm sensing you're not serious about working on your issues."

She jotted a note to remind herself to send Lester Boyle a letter explaining that his therapy was court ordered, and she was going to have to inform the court of his violation of that order.

"Nothing like telling a guy with a serious anger-management problem that you're ratting him out," she mumbled as she walked back through her bedroom to her bath and turned on the faucet. *Could this day suck any more?* she wondered as she prepared for her favorite indulgence.

As the Roman tub filled with hot, steamy water, she added a handful of lavender salts to the bath. Next, she lit the lavender-scented candles around the back ledge and went into her bedroom to retrieve the latest L. S. Connor novel, *Hide and Seek.* She placed the book on the tiled first step up to the tub. Next, she went into the kitchen to pour herself a glass of wine, returned to the bath to place it next to the book and then stripped off the rest of her clothes.

In no time she left her world behind, engrossed in the latest adventures of Connor's fictional hero, Caleb "Lucky" Wyatt. Wyatt was equal parts James Bond and Indiana Jones and Molly's personal guilty pleasure. The author's style was wonderful and the larger-than-life tales of Wyatt—head of ACE, the Anti-Crime Enforcement Agency—were both entertaining and romantic.

Yes, she was fully aware of the fact that she was living vicariously through a fictional hero—the kind that didn't exist in the real world. Yes, she knew that when Wyatt seduced a woman in the book it wasn't her. And that was a shame, because Wyatt was her ultimate fantasy man. He was intelligent, sexy, handsome, resourceful, cool under pressure, quick on his feet. He was—

A lot like Chandler Landry.

Molly almost dropped her coveted novel into the tub when that disturbing and unwelcomed parallel popped into her head.

Thinking carnal thoughts about a fake guy in a book was okay. It was safe. Equating Chandler to Wyatt was just wrong. Actually, merely thinking about Chandler in those terms was the total opposite of safe.

Aside from being a virtual stranger, he was everything she avoided in a man. There was the whole thing about his looks. It had been her experience that if the Good Lord gave a man physical perfection, he countered the generosity by subtracting important elements from other areas. Gorgeous men were usually arrogant. Usually self-possessed. Usually as shallow as a mud puddle after a long drought.

Then there was the money thing. Chandler—all the Landrys—were loaded. Old-family-money rich. The town of Jasper was founded by and named for Jasper Landry, Chandler's however-many-greats grandfather. Rich guys were different. Different rules, different standards. Not that she was impoverished, but Molly knew he was way out of her league.

Then there was the celebrity thing. Chandler was a version of local royalty. His life was public and Molly—perhaps above all else—valued her privacy. It was safer to guard her past than to have to answer painful and intrusive questions.

She read the papers. She knew that any woman associated with Chandler normally got a mention of some sort. "Not mention," she muttered as she put her book down and took a sip of wine. "A label," she continued, sarcastically recalling what she'd read. "Former model blah-blah, or disgraced debutante blah-blah. Pass, thanks."

She heard the phone ring in the bedroom but opted to let the machine pick up. She returned to her book and hated the fact that as she read her mind's eye pictured Chandler in the role of her beloved Wyatt.

IT WAS WELL AFTER MIDNIGHT when Chandler arrived at his family's ranch house. While he would always consider the place home, the huge clapboard house was currently occupied by his brothers Shane and Sam. But that was about to change. Sam and Callie were in the process of building their own place on the east edge of the property. Chandler guessed the decision to move out was two-fold. First and foremost, Sam and Callie had two kids and smart money said more would follow. Second, sharing living space with Shane probably cut into their private time. Assuming married people with two kids actually had private time.

Shane greeted him by opening the door wearing a deep scowl.

"Good evening," Chandler commented, unable to keep the brotherly taunt out of his tone.

"Not when you're stuck with the Housekeeper from Hell under your roof."

"I heard that!" came a familiar voice from just inside.

Soon Taylor Reese was just behind Shane, her small frame barely visible behind Shane's huge bulk.

"*You* drank the last of the milk, so *you* should be the one making the middle-of-the-night run to the store."

It was obvious that Taylor wasn't the least bit intimidated by Shane's size. In fact, Chandler was certain that if need be, Taylor would climb up on a box in order to slug his youngest brother if the mood hit. And judging by the dagger glances they exchanged, he wondered if some hitting might not be in the very near future.

"Shopping is part of *your* job description," Shane countered.

Taylor planted her hands on her slender hips. "I did shop. I just didn't know you'd be inconsiderate enough to drink the milk meant for the children who live under this roof. Notice I said children,"

Taylor continued. "Since you're the only baby that lives here." Taylor turned and walked away.

"I want you fired," Shane yelled at her retreating back as he stomped down the porch steps.

"Well," Taylor called over her shoulder, "I want you rendered mute, but as my grandma always says, wantin' ain't gettin'."

"Seth's in the kitchen," Shane said to Chandler as he passed. "Normally I'd say go on in and help yourself to some coffee, but you'd better run that past Taylor the Tyrant first."

Chandler was still chuckling as he entered and went to meet Seth. Taylor was nowhere to be seen, so he guessed she had retired to her room for the night.

Seth was seated at the kitchen table, poring over photos Chandler recognized as the crime-scene shots. After grabbing a beer from the fridge, he sat in his chair. No matter how old they got or how long they'd been away, each of the Landrys seemed to automatically fall into the chair assigned them as children.

"Thanks for coming," Seth said, looking up. "I figured it was closer to have you meet me out here than to drive to my office."

"No sweat," Chandler returned easily, twisting the top from the bottle and taking a long swallow. "What's up?"

"This," he said, sliding an eight-by-twelve color

photograph across the table. It was an enlargement of the mark they'd noticed on the body earlier. "Mean anything?"

Chandler studied the photograph. "A circle with the number thirteen in it. Looks like a burn."

Seth nodded. "The M.E. says it was branded into the skin post mortem."

"Well," Chandler let out a breath as his mind whirled. "It could be from a ranch in the area. Easy enough to check."

"I did that. Look at the size. Average brand is about three inches. This is smaller than a cattle brand, and there's no listing in the registries for a thirteen in a circle."

Chandler took a slug of beer. Unlucky thirteen. Could be anything. But somehow he knew there was a correlation…somewhere. "My station is carried on channel thirteen. Maybe Caller John just doesn't like WOM-TV 13." A chill of foreboding made the back of his neck itch. He wondered if Molly was asleep. She might have some insights on the whole thirteen thing. And he wouldn't exactly mind hearing the sound of her voice. To know she was okay, he reasoned. It had nothing to do with the fact that he found her incredibly attractive and interesting. He glanced at his watch. Twelve-fifteen. Too late to call—

Seth frowned as he pulled the photograph over to take another look. He glanced up, and Chandler could read the concern he saw in his brother's eyes. "Dislike for the station. Maybe. Or this guy was specifically sending a message to *you*."

"Unless that message is to convey he likes to dismember women, I'm not real clear on his meaning. Besides, why me? I'm not exactly a hated figure."

"Yeah, I know, you're adored by millions," Seth teased. "The M.E. enhanced the mark enough to discover an interesting detail."

"What?"

Seth turned the photo so Chandler could look at it again. "Look at this," he pointed to the inner edge of the circle. "See the tiny dots around the thirteen? Looks like this was a homemade branding iron. Copper most likely. Something someone soldered in their garage. And look at the edges of the brand. Iron was too hot according to the ME. And left on the skin for longer than the couple of seconds required to mark cattle. No rancher did this. At least not a competent one."

"Great," Chandler snorted, disgusted. "So we're looking for a guy who's good with tools. That narrows the field to pretty much anyone who lives in Montana."

"I need you to go back through your tapes. Maybe this guy has called you thirteen times before. Maybe you've mentioned a story thirteen times. Maybe—"

"Maybe," Chandler interrupted. "This has nothing to do with *me*. Have you thought of that?"

"Maybe it doesn't," Seth said flatly. "Maybe this sick jerk just branded thirteen on his mother—or whoever this woman actually is—for kicks. Then again, maybe it *does* have something to do with you." He got up to grab the coffeepot and brought it back to the table.

"He could just be a sicko who wanted to capture the moment in living color for posterity. Believe me, Seth, we gets lots of calls from people who are attention junkies. It's probably about him, I was probably just a randomly selected schmuck who happened to have open calls at the time he decided to kill. And there's still the big, as-yet-to-be-determined 'if.' We still don't know who Floater Jane is, so—"

"I'm willing to lay odds it's your caller's mother. But erring on the side of caution, remember that he called your station, your show. So directly or indirectly there must be *some* sort of correlation. Find out what you can back at the studio, okay? Coffee?"

Chandler shook his head, preferring to stick with his beer. Seth refilled his mug and set the pot on the table before sitting down again. "Nothing would please me more than knowing there's no connection to you. But I'm sure as hell not leaving any stones unturned until I know that answer for certain."

He and his brother shared one of those silent, meaningful moments that were as natural among the Landry brothers as breathing. Sure, they'd battled their way through childhood, fighting over little things as most siblings do. But he knew in his heart—as they all did—that Seth would have his back. "I'll get the info to you ASAP."

"Thanks. And I think we should ask—" Seth's words were cut off by the urgent beeping of his pager. "Speak of the devil."

"What devil?" Chandler demanded as the hair on the back of his neck rose.

He was halfway out of his chair when his brother said, "Molly. A patrol unit was just dispatched to her house. John made contact."

Chapter Four

"You'll be punished for not listening to me. Sleep well, Doc." It was the unmistakable voice of John, echoing through the house.

Rage surged through Chandler as he listened to the message for the third time. Silently he fought to keep from punching the girlie peach-colored wall above the foyer table. Judging by Molly's frazzled expression and trembling fingers, Chandler was pretty sure the very last thing she needed was a moment of purely macho idiocy from him.

But it sure would have felt good.

"Mind if we sit for a minute?" Seth asked, giving his brother a calm-down-right-now look.

Nice work if he could do it, Chandler thought.

Molly seemed momentarily confused, then smiled weakly as she raised her hand and ushered them further inside the modest town house.

If he thought the paint was girlie, it couldn't hold a candle to the combination living and dining rooms. It didn't take any crack investigative skills to see that a woman was the only occupant. The place was a swirl of peach and pink flowers. He felt like a fool when he took a seat on the sofa—if that's what it was. He was forced to share the diminutive, floral two-seater with his brother. It was a tight fit, and he wasn't feeling particularly friendly right now. He and Seth fit snuggly side by side, knees brushing the edge of the brass-and-glass oval coffee table that was just big enough for the china bowl filled with dried flowers. Next to the flowers— which he quickly realized were the cause of the subtle fragrance in the room—a stack of silver coasters stood in a precise tower.

"Tell me about the call," Seth prompted.

"I was in the tub," she began.

Chandler swallowed. Up to that point he'd been trying to ignore the fact that she was clad in a pale-pink, very clingy robe. Though it was knotted tightly at her waist and fell modestly to just above her knees, it was, in fact, covering her very naked body.

He was going to burn in hell. No ifs, ands or buts. This poor woman had done nothing but fill in on his show and all of a sudden she was caught in the crosshairs of some sicko. *And what am I doing?* his own voice sneered inside his head. Lusting. Big-time.

Molly sucked in a slow breath. It didn't help his

lust quotient. Nope. Not when the fabric pulled taut across her chest, leaving virtually nothing to his overactive imagination.

"I let the machine pick up," she continued.

He tried not to focus on the low, sensual cadence of her voice as it caressed his ears.

"I was reading, so I didn't get the message right away."

"That explains the delay," Seth remarked. "Is the time stamp accurate on the machine?"

She nodded. "But I already checked the caller ID, it was from a blocked number."

"If you give him permission, Seth can dump the LUDs."

She blinked, then directed those wide, gray-green eyes in his direction. He wanted to go to her and gather her in his arms. The old, me man, you woman, B.S. Ridiculous. As if she wasn't freaked out enough after the day she'd had.

Down boy, he cautioned his libido.

"LUDs?" she asked.

"Local usage details," Chandler supplied, relaxing a little. "Knowing the date and time of the call, the phone company can pinpoint where the call originated even from a blocked line."

His remark caused the concern to drain from her face. In its place, color returned, leaving her with a freshly washed glow that only seemed to heighten her attractiveness. Chandler made the fatal mistake of stealing a glance in his brother's direction. Maybe she wasn't picking up on his secret fantasies, but one look at Seth told him his brother knew full well what direction his thought processes had taken.

Chandler decided to ignore his brother for the moment and silently commanded his mind and body to refocus. "Is your home number listed?"

She shook her head, allowing a few strands of dark-blond hair to fall forward. She shoved them back off her face, then said, "No."

"But there was a message from one of your patients?" Seth prompted. "Do you give your home number to your patients."

"I have remote access to my office voice mail. That call from Mr. Boyle actually went to my office."

"How do you know the difference?"

She explained the system, then added, "I do give some patients my home number. It depends on the circumstances."

"So, your number *is* out there," Chandler concluded, rubbing the stubble on his chin.

"Selectively," she replied, a twinge of annoyance in her tone. "I treat a variety of patients. Some for years. I only give out my home number to those select few people I know don't pose a threat to me."

"Ever been wrong?" Chandler countered.

Her eyes narrowed slightly before she answered. "No. Not once."

He knew he couldn't make the same claim, so he wondered about the veracity of her statement but decided this wasn't the right time to challenge her.

"Mind if I look around?" Seth asked.

"For what?" she asked.

"I just want to check out the windows and locks, I'll have the officer who responded to your call do the exterior."

Seth's question seemed to drain some of the color from her face. "That's sweet of you. And yes, I'm careful never to leave anything unlocked, but a second pair of eyes never hurts. Especially not when I consider that John has already managed to get his hands on my unlisted, private number."

She rose, Seth stood, so Chandler did the same. He went along for the walk, not so much because he didn't think his brother was capable of securing her home, but just out of sheer curiosity. Besides, he knew that eventually, he'd get a grand tour of her bedroom, and he pretty much planned to savor that moment.

"…is all there is to it," she finished, leading the parade of very large Landry men into the private sanctuary of her bedroom.

Seth went directly to the window, whereas Chandler made a beeline directly to her bookcase. When he reached for her copy of *In Too Deep,* maybe her all-time favorite L. S. Connor novel, she had to swallow the urge to yell, "Don't touch that!" at his very impressive back.

Impressive wasn't a good enough word. Nope, not for Chandler Landry. A decent sale at her favorite boutique could be called impressive. This man needed something more, an adjective that captured his absolute, unfettered perfection. No wonder he had garnered fame in the Jasper dating world. Heck, in this world he was a god among mortals. At least when compared to her pretty average dating options. Molly wasn't a nun, but she truly couldn't remember ever having such an extreme emotional and physical reaction to a man. It was as though every fiber of her being had Chandler radar as she watched him flip through her most-prized possession.

Nerves still frazzled, adrenaline still pumping, she needed a distraction right now. And what better distraction than Chandler? She noted every detail—from his clothing to his expressively handsome face.

His jeans fit like a second denim skin, particularly around the thighs, where the fabric was worn and tight, encasing powerful legs that her brain instantly stripped naked.

Mentally scolding herself didn't seem to help. Nope, libido had saturated her intellect. She'd wanted a distraction from fear, and what better way than to replace it with lusty thoughts. Just because she was thinking about him naked didn't mean she had to act on that impulse. She just went with it. His hips and waist were narrow, but, given his height and the breadth of his massive shoulders, she was hard-pressed to classify him as anything other than huge.

Normally she would have considered that a definite deterrent. She wasn't usually attracted to large men, maybe because she didn't like feeling physically inferior to anyone. But tonight, as the clock on her bedside table rolled close to 2:00 a.m., had he crooked his finger in her direction, she would have taken a running jump.

She took an involuntary and protective step backward, almost touching the wall in her desire to put some distance between herself and the handsome image of Chandler running his fingertips over her coveted books.

She swallowed the lump of primal desire that was trying desperately to lodge in her dry throat. So what if he was more than six feet of chiseled perfection. It didn't matter that his eyes were a rich brown, flecked with just enough gold to elevate them out of the "ordinary" category. And the man had a great body, so great, in fact, that she was sure the mere memory would haunt her dreams.

"That does it," Seth said.

You have no idea, she thought, plastering as benign a smile on her face as possible.

"We'll be going, now," Seth continued, walking toward the second floor hallway.

"Unless you'd like me—uh, us to stay." Chandler offered.

Us? No. You? Bigger no. "I'm fine now," she insisted, flattening herself against the wall so that no part of his massive and appealing frame made contact with her.

He paused, looming large above her. He was close, close enough for her to feel the warm wash of his breath against her upturned face.

Speaking of breath, Molly was holding hers. A fact she was fairly sure wasn't lost on him. She based that on the slightly self-satisfied smile curling the right side of his mouth. She was embarrassed, more so when she felt the heat begin to warm her cheeks.

"I would be happy to stay with you tonight," Chandler offered in a smooth, inviting voice that had her knees threatening to buckle beneath her.

With some effort, she was able to level her gaze and keep her pleasant smile from slipping. Every cell in her body was screaming, "Yes! Stay! Me first!" but luckily her intellect had returned from its stroll down Chandler Lane. "Tonight is almost over and I have to be at my office by eight. But, thanks, anyway."

"SHE SHOT YOU DOWN, deal with it."

Chandler slammed the door of his brother's cruiser and glared at him by the dim light of the dashboard console. "My offer was sincere."

Seth snorted loudly. "Sincerely meant to separate her from her panties."

"I was being nice."

"Please, bro," Seth said as he steered out of the small community and turned west, back toward the Lucky 7 Ranch. "I knew letting you come with me was a bad idea. You were practically drooling over the poor woman."

"She is seriously droolworthy," Chandler insisted, his mind filling with images of Molly in her silky pink robe. "Did you see the legs? Incredible legs."

"Leading, eventually, to an incredible mind. Face it, Chandler, the woman is too smart to get involved with a guy like you."

"Thanks for the vote of confidence. What's that supposed to mean, anyway?"

"It means you're out of your league. Molly impresses me as a kind, compassionate woman who doesn't need you messing with her."

"When did I become a serial killer?" Chandler muttered. "I'm a decent guy. I've got—"

"An aversion to meaningful, interpersonal relationships. Face it, dear brother, you don't want any part of her. She's happily *ever* after, and you're happily *even* after."

"You're making me sound like a real jerk."

"I love you, Chandler. I'm your older brother and it's my job to tell you when you're about to make a huge mistake. Consider it said."

"And the mistake would be?"

"Setting your sights on a nice lady who has a serious problem just now. John—or whatever his real name turns out to be—has obviously fixated on her. Don't you think one stalker at a time is enough?"

"Stalker? Don't you think you're being a little harsh?"

"Okay, but you get the point. You're probably only interested in her because she's pretending not to be interested in you. You're predictable, Chandler. You always want the things you can't have. And once you get them, you get bored and move on."

"That's not true."

"Allison Janeway?"

He hadn't heard that name in years but still remembered the months of pleading phone calls and tearful scenes after he'd broken off with her. "She was an exception."

"Bethany Carter?"

Chandler winced. "She didn't take our parting well. But you can hardly blame me for the overreaction of those two women."

"Cynthia Felder."

Chandler felt annoyance knot in his gut. "Are you spewing these from memory, or did you keep a list?"

"Actually," Seth's tone indicated he was amused, "I was listing them alphabetically. Next comes, um, Debbie Gayle. Edie Hanover. Francine Smy—"

"I get it," Chandler cut in. "So maybe I'm just picky. Or I haven't met the right woman yet. Ever consider that?"

"Nope. Every one of the women you've dated have been great. I think—"

"Some of them were *not* great," Chandler argued. "You may have a long memory but it's pretty damned selective. Remember Shauna Bellows? She was a long way from great."

Seth chuckled. "But she loved you, Chandler. She desperately wanted to bear your children."

"Was that before or after she went to rehab for her secret pill habit?"

"Okay, so Shauna wasn't the best choice for a life partner. Face it, bro. The truth of the matter is you aren't ready for a life partner. Everything is still all about you."

"I don't recall you falling on your sword at your wedding reception. You're happily married, and no one ever thought that would happen. Look at Chance and Val. Who knew he'd ever succumb to wedded bliss. Hell, look at Clayton! Sam and Callie. We all thought Sam would never remarry after that disaster with Lynn and then he found Callie."

"Sam almost blew it by keeping his secret."

Chandler sighed. "Point. But my secret isn't like Sam's. And when I told you, you promised you'd never bring it up."

"I haven't told a single person," Seth said, pausing long enough to make a cross over his heart. "But I've never met a secret that didn't come back to bite somebody in the ass."

DRAGGING was the only way to describe the way Molly moved toward her door at 7:45 that morning. She was twisting the earphone connected to her cell into her ear while balancing her briefcase and a travel mug of hot coffee.

"Dammit!" she cried as the hot beverage splashed out on her hand as she turned the key and locked her door. The morning wasn't looking up as she might have liked.

As was her practice, Molly made phone calls during her drive. It was efficient and allowed her to make the best use of her time. She knew which of her friends were early risers, which ones got up late, and she selected the calls to return accordingly.

Slipping behind the wheel of her car, she settled all of her things into place, then pressed the preprogrammed button on her cell and laid it on the console between the seats.

"Hello?" Claire Esterhouse's voice was chipper, perky and just the thing she needed to jump-start a better mood.

"Hi. Sorry I didn't get back to you yesterday. I was—"

"On the news and everything," Claire interrupted. "Did you see that poor woman's torso yourself? Was it as disgusting as I imagine? Was it the guy who called when you were on TV's mother?"

"Let me know when it's my turn to talk," Molly teased.

She and Claire had known each other for years, been roommates for a while, as well. They were close friends separated by life. Claire was now married, had moved to Helena with her successful, pharmaceutical-salesman husband and was hoping to start a family. They got together whenever they could, but Molly still longed for the old days, when Claire was only a bedroom away.

"Stan and I couldn't believe it when we watched the tape. By the way, I taped the show with the hunky newsman, in case you'd like to see it."

"Not really," Molly admitted. She explained how many hours she had spent with Seth and Chandler reviewing the segment and looking for some insight to John's identity. Then she told Claire about the message John left on her machine.

"Ohmygod!" Claire cried, genuine concern in her voice. "Why didn't you call us? We could have come down."

"A hundred-mile round trip? I don't think so, but I appreciate the thought. Besides, Seth and Chandler came over and—"

"The hunky newsman was at your place? Please,

please tell me you stripped naked and had your way with him. Better yet, tell me *he* stripped naked and you have pictures."

"Only in my mind," Molly admitted. "Pathetic, huh?"

"Then we're both pathetic 'cause I'm getting a pretty intense mental image right now."

"Claire," Molly joked with pretend sternness, "remember your wonderful husband."

"All I have to remember is not to yell out 'Ohh Chandler, baby,' when I'm having a perfectly appropriate and normal fantasy during my next sexual encounter with my husband."

Molly laughed, and her mood lightened. "You are so bad."

"Forget me, tell me all about him. Is he as cute as the billboards and posters all over the place? And when are you going to see him again?"

"Yes and no."

"Good and fool! Jeez, Mol, the man is a walking, talking invitation to wild passion. Take a walk on the wild side, my friend."

"The last time I took that walk, I tripped and fell flat on my face," she said.

"So your last few relationships haven't worked out. That doesn't mean you stop trying."

"I haven't stopped," Molly insisted. "I'm just taking a leave of absence."

"Boring. You don't have to marry the guy. But as

a fully qualified, board-certified therapist, I'm strongly urging you to have mindless sex with him."

"Because that's always a great way to approach a relationship," Molly returned easily. "Besides, he's a Landry, Claire. Of *the* Landry Family. Of the wealthy and privileged Landrys. Forget being out of my league. He's out of my universe."

"What? You don't think you can love and be loved by a rich guy? Didn't I teach you anything during our years together?"

"He's a public figure, Claire. And I'm the Queen of Private. And this conversation is completely silly because I'm probably not going to see him ever again."

"Chicken."

She heard the click and bleep of an incoming call, then said, "Gotta run, I've got another call."

"Cowardly chicken."

Molly was still grinning when she tapped the button to catch the incoming call. "Dr. Jameson."

"Molly, dear, you didn't return my call last night."

"I'm sorry, Gavin," she said with genuine emotion. "Things got a little strange." She proceeded to fill him in on the details of her long night. As always her mentor and friend listened patiently as she told him everything.

Well, almost everything. She didn't share with him that Chandler had her libido on high alert. Nor did she intend to. Not that Gavin wouldn't have gladly listened, that was a given. He wouldn't have cared that she found Chandler mind-alteringly appealing. Gavin was the most polished man she'd ever known, with the social graces of royalty. They'd been colleagues and friends since her residency, but she wouldn't feel comfortable telling him about her fantasy love life. She pulled into the parking lot of the strip medical center where she kept her office.

"…someone to stay with you until they find this John character," Gavin advised. "I could call around and see if there is a suitable person who could act as your bodyguard until this matter is settled."

Molly began to gather up her briefcase, purse, abandoned and cooling coffee, and last, the cell phone. "That really isn't necessary. I'm sure once the sheriff gets the phone records, John will be caught, and this will be nothing more than a bad twenty-four-hour period in my life."

"You should be more cautious," Gavin warned. "Perhaps you should discontinue seeing patients until this unpleasantness passes."

"I thought about that," she admitted. "But it really shouldn't be a problem." Molly used her foot to kick her car door closed.

"Still, caution should be uppermost on your mind. I really can't apologize enough," Gavin continued. "I feel as though I bear some responsibility.

After all, you were filling in for me on that program."

"And we both know people like John can fixate on someone for no rational reason. I have faith in the sheriff."

"I suppose we have to leave it to the professionals," Gavin said, relenting.

"Yes, we do." She was hopping and trying to balance everything without dropping the phone. No amount of gymnastics seemed to help. Finally she said, "I'm here at the office and I need at least two fingers free in order to open the door."

"I understand. Please call me this afternoon. I do worry about you."

"I know and I appreciate it. Stop feeling guilty and I promise to give you a call after lunch."

Molly disconnected the call at the precise time she dropped the phone and her coffee. The travel mug hit the cement walkway, opened, then splashed dark coffee all over the leg of her beige silk pants. As if in slow motion, the earpiece ripped out of her head, then floated down and landed in the coffee beginning to pool at her feet.

She cursed, then shifted her purse and briefcase higher on her shoulder and bent down to save her phone from certain destruction. Sighing heavily, she kicked the mug along the pathway toward the etched-glass door with her nameplate affixed to the brick exterior of the building.

Molly reached out with her key to slip it in the lock. Instead of fitting neatly inside the knob, the pressure from her hand pushed the door open.

She *never* left her office unlocked. Ever.

Fear dropped on her like a wet, heavy blanket. She was about to turn and race to the office next door when she felt a large hand clamp down on her shoulder.

Chapter Five

Molly shrieked, spinning to find herself staring into the concerned face of Ken Ross, the CPA from the office next to hers. "I'm sorry, Dr. Jameson," he began, drawing his pale hands back toward his rail-thin frame. "I…I didn't mean to startle you."

She smiled as she gasped to restore breath to her body. Ken was a nice enough guy, but right now his presence was hardly comforting. He reminded Molly of a praying mantis. He was a tangle of long, thin arms and legs and stood preternaturally still whenever they stopped to chat.

Lifting her hand, she said, "It wasn't your fault. I was spooked by the door being open."

"I noticed that when I came in this morning," Ken said, his pale eyes conveying worry. "You never leave the door open. I was concerned. I've been listening for your car."

"I'm concerned, too," she admitted. And Ken's presence wasn't exactly comforting. If he was concerned, Molly thought with some annoyance, why hadn't *he* called the police when he'd realized she wasn't the one who'd opened the door? Because, she reminded herself, nonconfrontational Ken wouldn't dream of facing any kind of authority figure unless he absolutely *had* to.

Sweet though he may be, a strong breeze could blow him into the next county. Where he'd probably have a sneezing attack and reach into his shirt pocket for the ever-present bottle of nose spray he always had at the ready.

"Do you want me to go inside with you? Or should we call the authorities? There could be a burglar in there." Ken blanched, turning even whiter than normal at the mere thought of confrontation.

She glanced around the parking area and saw no strange cars. That was comforting. Few burglars used public transportation in their getaway. Next, she looked at the door. No signs of tampering, no one had jimmied the lock, the glass was intact. Another good sign.

"Maybe I didn't pull it all the way closed," she reasoned. "I was pretty upset yesterday afternoon."

"I can imagine," Ken sympathized. "I...I was watching WMON when that cretin called you. And then again when they did the story on the body found at Spawn Creek. I can't imagine being involved in anything so horrible." Ken finished his sentence before his body convulsed into a series of bone-jolting sneezes.

"I'm sure it's nothing," Molly said, hoping to calm her companion. Forget nasal spray. After more than two years of friendship, she was fairly sure Ken's symptoms were all psychosomatic. Ken was a dear, but he was afraid of some things and claimed allergies to all others. "Besides, between your sneezing and my shrieking, anyone who might have been inside would have run out by now. Right?"

Ken brought a perfectly folded handkerchief to his nose as the sneezing subsided. "Of course. That would make sense. I'm overreacting, as usual."

Molly placed her hand on his sleeve and gave a small squeeze. "We both are. Still, would you mind staying outside here while I go in?" She didn't relish the idea of going inside, but she also didn't want to call the police for a second time in mere hours.

"But outside, right?"

Manly answer. "Yes, Ken. Right here by the door. I'll just be a second and then we can both rest easy."

His head bobbed in a nervous nod.

Molly reached inside the door, her fingers fumbling along the wall for the switch. Light flooded the tidy reception area, and she saw nothing out of place. The magazines were neatly stacked on the table, the coffeepot was poised and ready to begin brewing on her command. Not a thing to raise her concern. She felt her shoulders relax as she stepped inside, depositing her purse and briefcase into one of four overstuffed chairs that ringed the coffee table. She smelled the floral scent of the air freshener she kept discreetly plugged into an out-of-the-way outlet and something else. Something both familiar and strange.

Stepping further into her suite, she headed directly for the inner door—the one leading to her private office. To her relief, it was locked. As it should have been. She kept drug samples in her cabinet. But locking the door wasn't just about the cache of prescription drugs. Her sessions were private, her patients needed to know that they could speak freely without wondering if and when someone might come barging inside.

What is that smell? She wondered again as she placed her key into the lock. She knew that smell. It was…what was it?

The minute she opened the door and turned on the light she remembered. It was the smell of death.

"TOUGH START TO THE DAY," Chandler remarked as he came up beside where Molly stood at the opened doors of the ambulance, holding Ken's clammy hand while the EMT placed an oxygen mask over his gasping mouth.

She eyed him suspiciously. "Why are you here?"

"Seth called me."

Genuine hurt registered in his incredible eyes. As

much as she didn't want to notice such things, she seemed incapable of controlling herself. Regardless of the circumstances, it was impossible not to notice him. Chandler was just too much of a presence to slip into the setting unnoticed.

Nor did the camera crew pulling into the crowded parking lot. "I can't believe you're doing a remote report on this." Molly stiffened. She dropped Ken's hand. Keeping her voice low but stern, she said, "I don't want any part of you advancing your career."

Her intention of spinning on her heels and marching away, back stiff, dignity intact, lasted less than a second.

Chandler grabbed her arm and somehow managed to steer her in the direction of the videographers.

"I'm not going to participate in your report," she insisted, giving a fruitless tug at her captured arm.

"Hey! Chandler!" one of the cameramen called.

But Chandler kept moving, until they reached a shiny red Lexus parked on the shoulder of the road just beyond the parking lot. Molly heard the telltale chirp of his car alarm and the headlights flashed in the brilliant sunlight.

"Will you please—"

He cut her off by pulling open the door and depositing her into the passenger's seat. He crouched down in front of her, effectively holding her captive in the small space.

The hurt she'd seen in his eyes was gone. Now his gaze was a dangerous mixture of emotion, paramount was anger. It flashed, hot and strong, in her direction.

"This isn't about me or my career. I came because I heard what happened and I wanted to make sure you were okay."

She stared up at him, barely seeing the flurry of activity that had turned the parking area into something that looked like a command post. "But you brought a crew."

His head tilted off to one side, allowing a few thick strands of jet-black hair to cross his deeply tanned forehead. "It's what I do," he said in a softer tone. "I have a responsibility to the viewers to cover this story."

"Don't let *me* get in the way of your responsibilities. Forget me," she continued, her voice rising along with her ire. "Think about Mrs. Zarnowski's family. I'm sure they'll be comforted knowing that the images of her body being removed by the coroner's office satisfied *your* responsibility to *your* legions of adoring fans."

"It's my job, Molly. And like it or not, the public does have a right to know that a brutal murder took place in their community."

She crossed her arms in front of her and offered her best scowl. "You're just a walking public service, aren't you?"

"I'm a reporter. Like it or not, this is something that needs to be reported."

"Don't let me keep you."

"I wasn't planning to." He tossed her the keys to his car. "Drive into town. I'll meet you at Seth's office as soon as I'm done."

"Excuse me?"

His smile stilled her breath. "Go on to Seth's office. I'll catch a ride there with someone."

"Why?"

"Because Seth needs to question you, and I have to go live in about three minutes."

"That isn't an explanation."

He let out a short breath, then rose to his full and imposing height. "If you're here on the scene and I don't get you on tape, Mike will ream me a new one. Even footage of you hiding your face would make it on air. I doubt you want that."

She nodded her agreement.

"I've got a job to do and I'll do it, but I'm not willing to plaster your face on my station a second time. Not while John is after you. So—" he paused, then reached forward and folded her fingers around his keys, then his fingers around hers "—go to the station. The deputies will make you comfortable until Seth and I get there."

Her anger melted away and she was left with an appreciative pool of emotion in the pit of her stomach as she watched him jog back toward the truck.

Gorgeous and considerate. Scary combination.

"At least our boy John is consistent," Seth remarked several hours later as they headed east into town.

Chandler agreed. John was a consistently bad guy. "And elusive. Didn't look like the crime-scene guys were having too much success back there."

His brother agreed, though Chandler could tell it annoyed him to do so. "Maybe the state lab can match the tool marks from the torso to the wounds on the victim in Molly's office. Maybe trace can come up with something." Seth slammed his palm against the car's steering wheel.

"I've got a bad feeling about this," Chandler said. "None of it makes sense."

"And murder is usually the first choice of a logical mind?"

Chandler peered out the window as they drove through town. He was running the possibilities, trying to find some thread to follow that would explain why a guy would call in to the show one morning and suddenly turn into a spree killer a few hours later.

They headed north on Mountain Road, passing Jasper Park to the left. Chandler was momentarily distracted by the activity in the park. It was a beautiful, unseasonably warm summer day. The sky was a bright blue and just a few clouds punctuated the mountains that guarded the historic little town founded by his ancestors. How he had missed this place during his years in the Middle East. Funny, at twenty-two, he couldn't wait to get out of Jasper, Montana. Back then he'd thought any place on earth would be more exciting than his hometown. Ten years later his entire perspective had changed. He'd raced back to Jasper, ready, willing and able to spend the rest of his life here.

His homecoming had been marred by more than just memories of war, an injury to his leg and a lack of direction. He'd been home less than a month when his mother and father had taken off for parts unknown. Well, kind of.

Chandler conjured the memory of his parents. Odd that, even now, after so much had happened, he still harbored secret hopes that they'd return soon. That hope had faded somewhat. He had no idea why his mother had abandoned her family and even less understanding of why his father had taken off to search for her without consulting any of his sons. He didn't know why—nor was he willing to forgive either parent for not contacting them over the years. He imagined them on a remote beach in Central America living out their golden years eating mangoes at the water's edge. It would have been a nice little scenario had it not been for the fact that until a few months ago, one of their sons had been in prison.

Clayton's trial had gotten lots of press. Enough so that their wayward parents should have been in contact. It didn't matter that Clayton had finally been exonerated; they should have come home. Just as they should have been there to welcome the newest generation of Landrys. They didn't know that Sam and Callie had two great kids and a third on the way; or that Seth and Savannah had a beautiful son, Wyatt, who had almost lost his life at birth. And by early next year, Clayton and Tory would welcome the next Landry into the fold.

"Earth to Chandler?"

He snapped back into the present just as Seth pulled the cruiser alongside the brick building that housed his office and the jail.

"Sorry, I guess I was taking a little mental nap."

Seth got out and adjusted his Stetson. "You're as transparent as a hooker's bra. You were thinking about the folks."

Chandler turned to stare at his brother. "How could you *possibly* know that?"

"Because every time you think of Mom and Pop your left cheek gets a tick."

He could have lied, but what was the point. Besides, Seth knew him too well. "We should find them." Chandler said when they'd both climbed from the car and up onto the curb. The aroma of bacon frying at the Cowboy Café across the street hung in the air.

"We've tried, remember?" Seth asked as he held open the heavy door to allow Chandler to enter first. "Obviously, they're in year eight of living off the hundred grand Pop took out of the bank. Until they use a credit card, we don't have a trail to follow."

"Some sheriff you are."

"Why don't you call Cody and rag him?" Seth tossed back. "He's a Fed. He's got more resources than I do."

"He's a Federal marshal not J. Edgar Hoover, Jr.," Chandler returned. "I doubt the attorney general is on his speed dial."

"I'll tell him you were mocking him the next time I talk to him."

"Tattletale," Chandler griped as he followed Seth through the swinging gate that was clearly marked Authorized Personnel Only.

Molly was sitting in a high-backed wooden chair, her small hands placed neatly in her lap.

Chandler read the strain around her eyes and in the tense lines at either side of her pretty lips. Poor woman, she'd had twenty-four hours from hell.

The blood in his veins pumped with a renewed sense of annoyance. No, more than annoyance. He was royally pissed.

"Thanks for waiting," Seth said, seeing them both inside his office.

"No problem. Should he be here?"

Chandler didn't like being relegated to a "he" but he let that pass.

"Chandler knows we aren't on the record here."

"We aren't?" she repeated, clearly surprised.

Seth smiled at her. "You and I are on the record Chandler is here because even though he's annoying, he's got a good head on his shoulders, and frankly I'll take all the help I can get to find this John character and put him behind bars. I need to ask you about Mrs. Zarnowski's murder."

After med school she'd prayed that she'd never again have to see another dead body. In the las twenty-four hours she'd seen two. Molly swallowed, hoping it might ease the queasy feeling in her stomach as she recalled the vivid image of her patient's body slumped in the chair. It didn't. Sitting in the worn leather chair opposite Seth didn' make it any better. But when Chandler's hand reached out and covered hers, she finally was able to find her way out of her ugly recall and back into the present.

"She was my first appointment," Molly explained Then, as soon as she said the words, she added, " had—have others today." She paused, pulled away from Chandler's touch, then rubbed her hand across her forehead. "I left so quickly I didn't even take my purse."

"Drove here without a license in your possession?" Seth asked.

Blinking twice, Molly realized she'd just admit ted to a crime. "I should have—"

Seth smiled as he interrupted, "I'm teasing you, Molly. Relax. The crime-scene techs will bring your things here in a little while. Chandler's idea to get you out of there was a good one. I don't want you doing anything to draw attention to yourself until we get a better handle on John."

"I've thought about him a lot. I swear, Sheriff Landry, I don't have anyone in my life capable of doing these things."

"Call me Seth, please. What about your line of work? Do any of your patients, um, have more screws loose than the others?"

"Well put," Chandler interjected. "Shows great insight and compassion on your part."

Molly found herself smiling. "It's okay," she promised. "My practice is pretty limited. I do family therapy and some court-ordered counseling. I don't do—"

"Court-ordered?" Chandler parroted.

Angling herself in the chair, she crossed her legs to make sure to cover the coffee stain, then leveled her eyes on Chandler. "Anger-management work. But none of my clients has any symptoms of the kind of person who would do these sort of things. I do a full personality work-up on each patient at the outset. I'd know if anyone was violent."

"Because they'd have a big *V* painted on their forehead?" Chandler challenged. "C'mon, Molly.

You can't tell if someone is violent just by looking at them."

She agreed, but she wasn't going to tell him that. "There are several indicators I look for when I begin treatment. Aside from anecdotal evidence of past rages or violent outbursts, I look for superficial charm." She clicked each item off on her finger as she spoke. "History of manipulative behavior, inflated sense of self, pathological lying, lack of remorse, shame or guilt, shallow emotional connections, inability to love, need for continuous stimulation, lack of empathy, poor impulse control, irresponsibility, promiscuous sexual behavior and—"

"I get it," Chandler held up his hands in mock surrender. "I wasn't questioning your thoroughness, Doctor. I was merely commenting that unfortunately for all of us, the bad guys are sometimes hard to pick out of a crowd."

"You don't have anyone who fits that profile?" Seth asked.

She shook her head. "And no new patients in over six months. My schedule is full, since I also teach at the university."

"Taylor used to work for you, right?" Chandler asked.

"She was my TA for a couple of years. Before she went to work for your family."

"Not my family exactly," Chandler corrected, a devilish smile threatening the corners of his mouth.

"She works for my brothers Shane and Sam. Shane, mostly."

"I know all about that," Molly admitted, finding the smile infectious. "Taylor doesn't keep her feelings for your brother much of a secret."

"She's definitely got his number," Chandler agreed, shifting his large body in order to extend his right leg.

Molly couldn't help noticing the odd way his leg didn't quite straighten. Was he injured? Had he recently undergone surgery? She reminded herself that it was none of her business and looked away.

"I think she's masking her true feelings by deflecting him with misdirected hostility."

Chandler's one brow arched. "Or as we lesser people say, she's screwing with his mind to keep from—"

"We get the point," Seth interjected. "While the interplay between our youngest brother and the housekeeper is amusing, I really need to ask you some questions. Would you like something to drink before we start?"

"I had several cups of coffee while I was waiting. I'm fine."

"Great." Seth shuffled some files on his cluttered desk and then opened a small notepad, pencil poised above it as his gaze settled on her.

Molly might have found it disconcerting had it not been for the fact that she was mildly distracted by the scent of Chandler's cologne. It was a manly mix of woodsy something that seemed to ignite her senses. Though she kept her attention fixed on Seth, every other part of her was homed in on Chandler. She could almost feel the heat of his large body next to hers. The sound of his breathing sidetracked her, as did her complete awareness of him. It was as if her body had some finely tuned new alarm that alerted every time he so much as moved a finger. It was quite bothersome.

"Tell me about your patient."

"Mrs. Zarnowski was—" she hesitated, knowing she was bound by doctor patient privilege. Somehow, privilege didn't seem to matter when she recalled how viciously the poor woman had been killed. "She suffered with depression. It became worse after the birth of her third child. I've been treating her for almost two years."

"Regularly?"

"Yes. Every Wednesday."

Seth scribbled some notes, then asked, "I don't think there's much chance this isn't related to the other murder. Just in case, how's her family life?"

"Her husband is totally supportive," Molly explained. "She also has two sisters who help— helped her with the children. I've had sessions with the entire family and I can't imagine any of them hurting her."

"I'll have to check it out, but thanks," Seth said. "Knowing that will make my job easier. I don't want to come down on the husband if you think he's a stand-up guy."

"He is," Molly promised. Suddenly her brain flashed an image. "Her car was in the lot."

"The green Buick." Seth nodded after checking his notations. "We ran the plate at the scene."

"I should have realized her car was there. I looked right past it when I found the door unlocked."

"Unlocked?" The question came from Chandler.

Seth's chair squeaked on its rollers as he sat back stroking his chin. "Assuming it was John, he may have been lying in wait for you and killed your patient instead."

Fear. Dread. Anxiety. Guilt. Every bad emotion she could name seemed to settle like a rock in her stomach. "I was about five minutes late this morning," Molly admitted. "But that doesn't explain how he opened the office."

"Is there any chance you could have left the door unlocked?"

She hesitated, then said, "Possibly, but highly unlikely. It has a dead bolt lock. I have to use the key, and I'm about ninety-nine percent certain I did that yesterday when I left."

"Who else has keys?"

Molly thought for a second before responding. "The cleaning company. Ferris Cleaning. Um, my friend Claire. We used to share the office space until she moved to Helena after her marriage. My friend Gavin. He's the head of my department and—"

"The guy who normally does the segment on my show," Chandler finished.

"I had a few deliveries during nonoffice hours, so I gave keys to Ken, the CPA next door."

"The guy hyperventilating at the scene?"

Molly nodded. "And the allergist two doors down. I left a key with him last winter when I was on vacation. Dr. Todd Warner."

"That's a lot of keys," Chandler commented.

"And Taylor," Molly added. Saying it out loud made her sound terribly irresponsible. It wasn't over yet. "And Rachel. She's my teaching assistant now. Rachel Mitchell."

"We can run them down," Seth said, offering her a smile.

"I trust all of those people," Molly insisted. "With the exception of Rachel, I've known them all *really* well for years. I'm not accusing Rachel of anything," she amended quickly. "She's been with me since Taylor left, and I trust her completely."

"I can find her at the university?"

Molly nodded. "But you're wasting your time. I really can't imagine that Rachel would do anything to help a guy like John. I mean, I don't think she's even had five dates in the past year."

Chandler touched her arm for a second. The shock of it threatened to send Molly jumping from her chair. "Before, when you were reeling off the attributes of a sociopath, you mentioned superficial charm?"

"Yes." Molly's brain kicked back into gear. "You think John might have charmed her into giving her the key to my office."

"It's a good lead," Chandler agreed.

She turned and studied his face quickly before asking, "How did you know I was reeling off the pathology of sociopathy?"

"I read a little, remember?" he answered, flashing that perfect-teeth smile at her.

Heat warmed her face and, fearing she'd blush as red as a tomato, she turned back and stared into her lap, hoping and praying the girlish reaction would fade quickly.

"What about the number thirteen?" Seth asked.

"Thirteen?" Molly repeated, and then allowed her mind to go wherever it pleased. "Unlucky thirteen? My grandmother used to make thirteen-bean soup. There are thirteen stripes on the American flag. Thirteen is the atomic number of aluminum."

"Good free association," Chandler remarked, teasingly. "What's thirteen-bean soup?"

She cast him a glance. "A soup with thirteen different beans in it. Why? What's the significance of thirteen?"

Seth cleared his throat. "The torso from yesterday had a burn on it with the number thirteen. And, well…"

"Well what?"

Chandler cautiously slid his hand back over hers, then said, "The killer stabbed Mrs. Zarnowski thirteen times before slitting her throat."

Chapter Six

Seth dropped another bombshell before she'd recovered from hearing the grisly details of her patient's untimely demise.

"There was a note under Mrs. Zarnowski's body."

"God." Molly pressed a hand to her stomach, then leaned forward in her seat. "What did it say?"

"John wants you to go back on television so he can talk to you."

Her stomach turned. Lurched, actually. The mere notion that some violent predator was giving her directions as if she was some sort of puppet was disconcerting to say the least. Especially knowing what he'd done to at least two women that they knew of, in the past twenty-four hours.

"He probably wants to see your face," Chandler added. "See what effect his murders are having on you. But if you want my two cents," Chandler snapped at his brother, "no way in hell is Molly going back on air so this sicko can see her face across a twenty-four-inch screen and gauge her re-action to these murders."

"I didn't ask her to do so," Seth said, looking a little surprised at his brother's outburst. "I just re-peated what was in the note."

Thanks, that helps. I'm not freaked out. "This makes no sense," she insisted, standing to pace in the small confines of Seth's office "I truly don't have this kind of enemy in my life."

"What kind do you have?" Chandler asked.

She shook her head. "I didn't mean it like that. Forget enemies. I don't have that many close friends. Unlike you, I'm a very private person."

"Or," Seth countered, "he could be targeting Chandler."

Molly stopped and regarded the younger of the two brothers. Now, that made some sense. It made sense, but her stomach still clenched. As strongly as she didn't want to be the target of somebody's hatred, she didn't want that kind of psychopathic behavior directed at Chandler, either.

But it did make some sort of twisted, creepy sense. Chandler was on television, the perfect me-dium to attract the fixation of some unbalanced soul. "And your show is on channel thirteen. Your image is in homes almost every day."

"And the note was addressed to him."

Seth's revelation stunned her. "To Chandler?"

The sheriff nodded. "But we're holding that back.

Once this story gets into the media, all sorts of crazies—sorry—come out of the woodwork. The note will be how we weed out the nut jobs—sorry again—from true leads."

"So, I'm not the target," she insisted, then pointed at Chandler. "He is."

Seth shrugged. While the gesture seemed casual and unconcerned, as someone trained to read body language, Molly could see that the sheriff was extremely concerned. "We don't know yet."

Annoyance and anxiety enveloped her entire body. It wasn't Seth's fault; he was doing what he could. But the impotence of just *waiting* was stretching her nerves. "When *will* you know?" she asked as calmly as her internal voice screamed.

"When we catch him, or when he makes his next move."

Not exactly comforting. "So we just wait?"

"With appropriate protection," Seth explained.

Her shoulders slumped forward. "What does that mean?"

"A deputy will be with you."

"It's for your own protection," Chandler added.

"That goes for you, too," Seth told his brother.

Molly heard his derisive snort. "Like hell. I can take care of myself."

"How very macho and stupid," Molly remarked, though secretly she shared some of the sentiment. She didn't relish the thought of having a stranger shadowing her, every waking hour. But unlike Chandler she wasn't a fool. If this man was after either of them, having an armed deputy close by would make her feel a lot safer. It might also prove to be a deterrent.

The thought that it might *not* made her press her hand to her midriff.

"This isn't up for debate," Seth continued. "The two of you will have protection round the clock."

Stepping forward, Molly placed her fingertips against the smooth surface of the desk and leaned closer to Seth. "There has to be a better system. My patients will not like having an armed guard in the waiting room. My students won't listen to word one of my lectures with a deputy present. We have to come up with a better plan."

"Sorry," Seth replied.

She could tell that he wasn't sorry in the least. She saw the determined set of his chin and realized she was fighting a losing battle. So she switched gears. "Can we set some parameters?"

Chandler gave her a hard look. "No."

"Such as?" Seth asked, overriding Chandler's knee-jerk answer to the question not directed to him.

"I don't want anyone in uniform, and I don't want any of my patients questioned."

"Plainclothes will be fine. But if there's something suspicious about a patient—"

"There won't be. Second, I don't want anyone in my house."

"Molly," Chandler began, "that isn't reasonable."

"Sure it is."

"No," Chandler insisted, standing to tower over her. "It isn't. Your town house has two points of entry. Playing by your rules would mean utilizing two officers, one for the front, one at the back. This isn't Helena, Molly. Seth only has five deputies, so you'll have to suck it up and let a deputy bunk on your couch."

"And you don't have a problem with all this?"

"We aren't talking about me, but no." He flashed her an amazingly annoying grin. "I don't have a problem because I'm not accepting any protective detail."

"That's stupid. What if you really *are* John's target?"

Chandler rolled his eyes. "Then John will be sorry. I can handle myself."

"I'll just sit back and listen," Seth said, his voice tinged with amusement. "Let me know when the two of you are finished."

"I think your overconfident, testosterone-addled brain is affecting your decision-making ability," she insisted above the sound of her anger pounding in her ears. "This isn't a litmus test of your manliness, Chandler. John is obviously an organized killer who plans his kills with militaristic precision." She had a sudden insight. "Maybe he's military. Or ex-military. He sounds young, but that doesn't mean he couldn't have been trained by or served in the armed forces for a couple of years. Maybe he was dishonorably discharged. That would make sense if he's as unstable as his actions imply."

"I'm already checking that angle," Seth said.

"If he was in the military, he probably has a history of trouble. His anger toward authority figures was apparent in his phone call to the TV station. He would have had great difficulty following orders."

"That happens," Chandler commented, almost sarcastically.

Molly felt her eyes narrow as she glared up at him. "I'm trying to help here and you're mocking me. In case you've forgotten, I am an expert on human behavior."

"But," Seth inserted, "he's the one with the military expertise."

"Wh-what?" Molly stammered.

Seth came around and draped a brotherly arm across Chandler's broad shoulders. "He doesn't like to talk about it—which is true of many aspects of his life." Seth paused as Chandler delivered an elbow to his ribs. "Ow. Chandler was Special Forces, Molly. Desert Storm, Rwanda, Mogadishu. Has a whole drawerful of medals and a bullet in his leg to prove it."

"No big deal," Chandler dismissed.

Molly knew better. She'd counseled a few veterans and knew a little about the horrors faced by the soldiers in combat. "I had no idea. I'm sorry for—"

"Forget it," Chandler insisted. "And you," he added, poking his brother's chest, "can forget sending any of your deputies along with me. I can handle myself. I've got to get to the station."

"I wish you'd reconsider," Seth argued, albeit halfheartedly.

"Wishing won't make it so," Chandler said before heading out the door.

His departure left a huge void in the room. Molly pushed that thought out of her head and retook her seat. Chandler was a puzzle. A complicated, gorgeous puzzle. Damn! Just what she didn't need just now.

"Listen, Molly," Seth began, "I know your files are confidential, but it would really help if you could let me take a look at—"

"Not possible," she told him. "I'm sorry. I can't break confidence, Seth. You know that."

"I'll accept it, for now. But I'm leaving that door open."

His tone and smile were equally reasonable, so she agreed. "I won't let you go through them, but I'll certainly begin doing it myself."

"Start with the court-ordered cases," he suggested. "I doubt John suddenly decided on a life of crime. You've probably had contact with him—"

"Assuming I'm the target and not Chandler," she

reminded him. "It actually makes more sense for him to have an issue with your brother. He's the public figure."

"To a degree," Seth remarked.

Degree? she silently wondered. Odd way to describe a man who, when he wasn't on air, had his image plastered all over the place in ads and promotions for the station. Chandler Landry couldn't have any secrets, his life was too communal for that to be a reasonable possibility.

Seth was smiling at her. "What? You don't think a TV reporter can have a private side?"

"I think it would be…difficult," she admitted. Molly was choosing her words carefully; after all, the sheriff was Chandler's brother.

He gave her a far too innocent look as he said mildly, "People aren't always what they seem on the surface."

"I know that better than most." She narrowed her eyes. "Wait. Are you insinuating that your brother leads some sort of secret life?"

Seth laced his fingers behind his neck and gave the appearance of complete ease. Except for the twinkle she saw in his eyes. *What did that mean?*

She shouldn't care. She didn't. Right? Wrong, her brain answered as she asked her question. "Does he have some deep secret?"

"Landry family ties prevent me from commenting one way or another," Seth replied easily. "We don't tell tales out of school."

"But there is a tale to be told?"

Seth simply shrugged. "Chandler's a complicated man. Probably the smartest of the lot of us. But I'll deny I ever said that if you repeat it to him."

"I won't. Besides, your comment implies that I'll have reason to speak to your brother again, and frankly I don't see that happening."

"Except for this whole John thing."

Molly felt a chill tingle the entire length of her spine. "There is that," she admitted. "But any conversations we have regarding John wouldn't include topics of a more…intimate nature."

Seth tossed his head back and laughed. "Good luck with that, Doc. I'll break the family code long enough to tell you that Chandler has set his sights on you. He can be an unrelenting cuss when he thinks he wants something."

Thinks he wants something? Was that some none-too-subtle way of letting her know she wasn't Landry-worthy? Well, they could all rot! She may not have more money than God, or a multigenerational pedigree, but she wasn't exactly pond scum.

She stood with the dignity befitting a queen, then said, "Will there be anything else?"

"Hang on," Seth scrambled to her side. "I said that wrong. I was just offering a friendly warning. Chandler is a great guy and he'd be lucky to have someone like you in his life. Hell, any man would be. Except me, of course. I'm a happily married man."

Her ire subsided. By force of habit, she began to analyze her reaction. Overreaction was a better word. She'd gotten all prickly because…why? "It doesn't matter," Molly insisted, hoping to end this strange conversation. "I'm not interested in Chandler, so he'll just have to redirect his sights."

"That was my point. My brother doesn't give up easily, and, well, I like you, Doc. You've been really decent to my family. You were a huge help with Kevin. I know how hard you worked to help him understand his kidnapping. He doesn't have a single scar or maladjusted moment."

She recalled the darling tow-headed little boy who'd been thrust into a difficult situation. Though there was always the possibility that he'd have issues later, thus far, he'd shown an amazing resilience. Possibly—in part at least—the large and loving environment created by the Landry clan. "He's a wonderful little kid."

"Agreed. And in many ways so is Chandler."

Not so little, she thought. "A kid? Your brother?"

"Just in some respects," Seth continued hurriedly. "Chandler is a deep, thoughtful guy a lot of the time but he's also the poster child for instant gratification. I love him more than life, but, well, his track record with women isn't so hot."

Yeah, like she needed that news flash. "His reputation is quite well…documented."

"He bores easily," Seth explained. "When it comes to women, he has the attention span of a water gnat. He likes the chase. I shouldn't be saying all this. I really only wanted to give you a heads up."

"My head is always up," she promised him. "And for your information, I crossed him off my potential date list about six seconds after we met."

Seth seemed to be struggling to keep from laughing. "I kinda figured that. However, with my brother, that's like wearing a big sign that says Try Harder."

"I'm sure he's a nice guy, but stop worrying, Sheriff. I can say no with the best of them."

"Good luck." The telephone on his desk rang. He spoke—grunted actually—for a few seconds, then said, "You can pick your stuff up out in the reception area. But your office is still being processed. Deputy McClain will be escorting you home or wherever you have to go."

"Home," she announced rather forcefully. "I don't have any classes today, so I think I'd like to go home and relax."

"Good idea," Seth agreed. "If you'd like, I can arrange for a specialized cleaning crew to go to your office."

"Don't go to any trouble. I can just call Ferris and have *them* take care of it."

His expression grew solemn. "You can, but the company I was talking about has expertise in cleaning up crime scenes."

Molly shivered. "Right. Yes. Okay."

Seth placed his hand on her shoulder. "I know this has been tough. We'll catch him, Molly."

THE DEPUTY ASSIGNED TO HER was a mannish-looking woman Molly put somewhere in the vicinity of her late twenties. Her hair was short—shaved at the nape, in fact. She had a reluctant smile and an air of efficiency that Molly appreciated, given the circumstances. Though she didn't talk much, the deputy was a woman of decisive action. When they went by to retrieve Molly's car, the deputy went over it with a fine-tooth comb. She checked under the hood, used what looked like a gigantic dentist's mirror to check the undercarriage, then finally announced it was safe for Molly to drive.

Once in the familiar interior of her car, Molly glanced down at her suit. It was the second casualty of the day. Along with the coffee stains, she now had the remnants of fingerprint dust smudged everywhere her purse and briefcase had touched.

The day was slipping away, as well. The last splinters of sunlight were fast sinking behind the mountain as she drove back toward her home.

She'd barely exited the parking lot—which was still home to several crime scene vans—when her cell phone rang. Blindly, Molly felt around in her purse until she found the phone, then brought it to her ear. "Hello?"

"Please tell me you are all right." Gavin's concerned voice crackled in her ear. "I've been calling you for hours."

"I'm fine, but I didn't have my phone with me." She filled him in on the events of the day.

"It would have been nice if one of the officers had answered the cell phone just to let me know you weren't available," Gavin complained.

"It was in the lab," she explained. "It probably didn't ring. You know the cell service rarely works inside buildings."

"Something I believe should be addressed by the regulators."

Only Gavin could make the lack of sufficient cell booster towers sound like a matter of national concern. "Hang on while I find my earpiece," she said, digging into her dust-covered bag for the accessory. After connecting it, she twisted the bud into her ear and placed the phone in the cup holder built in to the console. "So, how was *your* day?"

"This is not a time for levity," Gavin scolded. "I will now insist that you hire professional security. Additionally, I have arranged for your TA to cover all your classes until this…this *animal* is apprehended."

"First, I don't need private security, I've got a deputy glued to me for the foreseeable future."

"That is a good start, but I know you, Molly. You won't allow a strange man into—"

"A deputy of the female persuasion."

"A woman?"

Molly thought about the person tailing her home. "Yes, one I wouldn't want to meet up with in a dark alley. Believe me, if John shows up, I want this kind of woman between me and him. And Rachel doesn't need to cover my lectures, Gavin. I've already decided to cancel my appointments for the rest of the week. If I don't teach, I won't have anything to do until Monday, and I'll go stir-crazy with all that free time on my hands."

"I'm sure you can find some way to occupy your time. But as your friend and the head of the department, I have to consider the safety of everyone. We simply cannot put the students at risk."

"You're right, of course." Molly felt her spirits sinking. "I suppose I can find a few things to keep busy."

"I could come over," Gavin offered. "In fact, knowing you, you haven't eaten. Why don't I pick up dinner from that wretched barbecue place you're so fond of frequenting and come to your house?"

Dear, snobbish Gavin. He detested any meal that could be eaten with the fingers. The fact that he was willing to break ribs with her made it impossible for her to say no. "I'll be home in about ten minutes. Give me time to change. Say, sevenish?"

"I shall arrive bearing a most unhealthy meal and a bottle of wine that—did it have a conscience—would be embarrassed to share a table with a foil-wrapped slab of meat."

Molly smiled. "Lighten up, Gavin. And get extra sauce."

"Fine."

"And slaw. Don't forget the slaw."

"I wouldn't dream of it. No decent meal is complete without slaw."

She was still smiling as she pulled into her parking spot, followed almost instantly by the SUV driven by the officer.

"I'll go in first," McClain said as Molly stepped from her car. "Just hang back until I give you the all clear."

How could she have forgotten about the deputy? She nodded an acknowledgment of the woman's comment and then hit the redial button on her cell phone. Gavin's line was busy. Knowing his efficiency, he was probably already placing the order. For two. Well, she would wait a few minutes and call the restaurant herself to add sufficient food to the order to feed the deputy.

She was in the process of tugging her briefcase off the seat when she heard a large bang.

Then everything went black.

Chapter Seven

"Is she okay?" Chandler demanded over the raging sound of his heartbeat pounding in his ears.

Seth looked up, his face etched with concern. "Molly's understandably shaken up."

"And the deputy?"

His brother replied, "A concussion, minor burns on the right side and something about her eardrum."

Chandler surveyed the scene and wondered how anyone had survived the blast. Molly's town house was little more than a pile of smoldering rubble. "Where were they taken?"

"Community Hospital," Seth answered, squatting in order to poke the tip of his pen around a metal object nestled among the debris. "Chance is on call. He's supposed to get back to me with an update as soon as he checks them out."

"Smell that?" Chandler asked, sucking in a deep breath to confirm his suspicions. "C-4. No one uses C-4 anymore."

Seth stood, shoving the Stetson back on his forehead. "It's available on the black market."

"Did you call ATF?"

Seth nodded. "We'll send them samples, but C-4 isn't like having ballistics. All they'll be able to do is confirm what we already know."

Needing to expend some of his anger, Chandler went over and kicked at the charred remnants of Molly's sofa. He let out an expletive as the wooden frame splintered into fragments. None of this made any sense. Including the overwhelming sense of responsibility choking him. On a purely intellectual level, he knew he wasn't personally responsible for the present circumstances, but that didn't seem to assuage his guilt.

Molly had gone on his show of her own volition. Still, he needed only to conjure the image of her face to feel a renewal of emotion.

"This must be about her," he told Seth when he'd composed himself enough to speak in a normal tone.

"Or John just wants us to think that and you're the target."

"I didn't get blown up."

"Thankfully," Seth said, his tone serious, "neither did she."

"IS SHE REALLY OKAY?" Molly asked for the third time.

Val Landry smiled; a reassuring and honest expression that seemed to suit the very attractive, very pregnant woman. Val was a pretty brunette with an almost exotic look. And Molly didn't need a degree to see that she adored the husband at her side.

Molly experienced that small pang of jealousy that normal single women felt when in the presence of normal happily married women. Not a bad kind of envy, just that momentary what-if wondering while in the company of someone who had taken a different path in life.

Molly had chosen to focus on her career. And there were perks to the single life. She didn't have to account for her time; her schedule was her own. She had the freedom to do anything or go anywhere without worrying about or incorporating anyone else's likes or dislikes into her decision making. She wasn't responsible for anyone else's happiness. And she knew from painful experience what a burden it could be to arrange your life around the needs of another human being.

But, Molly secretly acknowledged, as Val continued to clean the abrasions she'd suffered in the explosion, her autonomy came at a price. Loneliness. It would be nice to have someone to share things with. Someone who knew her. Completely. The way Val seemed to anticipate her husband's needs and actions without a single word passing between them. All during Chance's examination of her, Val had known when to hand him what.

Then there were those moments reserved for couples; the brushing of hands, the touching of fingers—important non-verbal communication. Completely comfortable, unguarded moments that played out like an expertly choreographed dance.

"Chandler is on his way," Val said after answering the telephone mounted on the wall by the door.

"Why?"

Val absently massaged her distended abdomen. "The family rumor mill has it that he's got a thing for you."

Molly raised a brow. "In less than two days?"

"Landrys are men of action," Val reasoned. "When they aren't being complete *fools.*"

Molly smiled for the first time in hours. "That doesn't sound like upholding the party line."

"Just wait, you'll see what I mean. But don't get me wrong." Val paused long enough to dab some antiseptic-smelling, very cold liquid on the scrape to Molly's forearm. "All of them are wonderful men, but they seem to falter when it comes to matters of the heart."

"My heart isn't involved."

"Give it time," Val promised. "You say that now, but wait until you've kissed him."

Molly's heart stopped for a second. *Kiss him?* Not going to happen. "Since kissing isn't in the plan, I should be fine."

"May not be in *your* plan, but I'm sure it's in *his.*"

"Plans are made to be broken." Molly stiffened,

sitting very straight on the edge of the gurney. Her movement caused the paper sheet covering the bed to crinkle loudly.

"This ought to be fun," Val said, her eyes glinting with amusement. "Good for you. Give Chandler a run for his money."

"I'm not interested in him or his mon—"

The door swung open and slapped the wall, then Chandler's presence overwhelmed the small space. Though she'd seen a lot of him over the past few days, his incredibly handsome face still managed to quicken her pulse.

Val leaned next to her ear and whispered, "I hate to break it to you, but you sure *look* interested for somebody who isn't interested."

"How is she?" he asked Val as he swooped into the room with the force of a cyclone.

"She's doing fine," Val told him briskly as she put away her supplies and tidied up. "Lacerations, a second-degree burn on her ar—"

Molly waved a hand. "Hello you two? *She's* sitting right here fully conscious."

Chandler turned his gaze on her. Scanning her from her sooty forehead to her dirty bare toes peeking from beneath her crinkly paper blanket. "How do you feel?"

"Not bad, all things considered." Molly did her best to keep her expression bland even as she felt a jolt of heat as he gently picked up her left hand and cradled it in his. He examined first her palm, then the back of her hand, one finger at a time, checking the minor injuries she'd sustained. Molly stared down at his large strong hand supporting hers, and the jolt skittered through her system like heat lightning.

He picked up her other hand and inspected a particularly bad burn that glistened with the salve Val had just applied. His face was so close to hers that she could feel his breath, smell the musk of his cologne. Molly was grateful she wasn't hooked up to a monitor, which at this point would be beeping like crazy as her heart rate spiked. His lashes flickered up as he met her gaze. "I'm sorry you were hurt," he whispered a breath away from her mouth.

Mouth dry, Molly tried for nonchalance. "It could've been worse. I'm really okay."

His face openly registered genuine relief once satisfied that she truly had come away from the explosion with hardly a scratch.

So what if every cell in her body convulsed when his lips grazed her forehead. It was probably just a delayed—if intense—reaction to the events of the past few days. Yes! That would explain why she was literally reduced to a pile of quivering hormones in the presence of the opposite sex for the first time since high school. *Sex?* Why did she have to think that word?

"I can't believe you're okay."

I can't believe I want to rip off my clothes and have my way with you right here.

"I'll go do the paperwork to spring you," Val said. "And nice to see you too, Chandler."

Somewhat reluctantly, he stepped back to place a kiss on Val's cheek. "Sorry. How's my favorite sister-in-law?"

"Fat. Tired. This baby is making me very cranky."

Chandler put a hand on Val's belly. "Don't listen to her," he called to the unborn child. "She's always been cranky."

Val swatted him away. "Give me five minutes, then she's all yours."

Molly wasn't sure how to feel about being passed off so easily. Why did every Landry think she would so easily integrate herself into the menagerie? As welcoming as it might be, she wasn't a big-family kinda girl. And nothing she'd learned thus far had changed that opinion. There wasn't any privacy in Landry Land. Everyone seemed to know everyone else's business.

"I don't know why you came," she said as soon as Val had left them alone. "I'm quite capable of—"

"I was worried."

Tilting her head back, she met his gaze. It was an intense and disconcerting experience. *Why?* Because his eyes were dark, mysterious pools that she could easily get lost in? Or because just the thought that he might pull her into his arms was so intriguing she might beg him to do it?

This was crazy. Molly didn't swoon, yet that was the best way she could describe the unfamiliar sensations pelting her consciousness. Her palms felt sweaty, and her heart rate wasn't quite regular. Yep, she had all the signs of a woman ready to keel over at the mere sight of a man. So why this man? And why now?

"We're in the middle of an extreme situation," she explained, glad that her voice didn't crack along with the final remnants of her self-control. "Often that leads to extreme feelings and reactions that we otherwise wouldn't act upon. While I appreciate your concern, we have to acknowledge that this...*situation* isn't conducive to beginning a relationship."

His lips curved into an amused grin that made her blood pressure spike. "What?" she demanded, more forcefully than she might have liked.

He shook his dark head, but the smile remained annoyingly in place. "Please, feel free to psycho-analyze my motivations at will."

"That's what I do," she reminded him.

"There are some things you just feel, Molly. You don't think about them."

"Maybe you don't," she promised him, not bothering to hide the accusation in her tone. "You can't possibly claim to feel anything for me. You don't know me and I certainly don't know you."

Chandler moved and hoisted his very large body up next to her on the gurney. Not a great solution for her. Molly was engulfed by the appealing scent of his cologne. She was too aware of the heat emanating from him. And the heat his closeness inspired in her. So what was the alternative? If she jumped down and ran away, she'd be the jerk. Chandler was not going to make a fool out of her. Not now. Not ever.

"What do you want to know?"

She blinked. "Wh-what?"

"Ask me anything. If your objection to my honest display of concern is based on the idiotic claim that you don't know me, then ask me some questions. *Get* to know me."

Did he call me an idiot? The paper covering crinkled beneath her hands as she shifted in order to look up at him. "That was rude."

"That was my intention," he admitted without apology. "You're the one with the hang-ups, Doc. I think rushing over to the hospital to check on you after your house was blown to bits should have earned me a smile, not a lecture on interpersonal relationships."

"From what I hear," Molly told him wryly, "the only thing you know about interpersonal relationships is how to avoid them."

"True." Again he didn't seem to care that his admission wasn't exactly going to earn him Brownie points.

"Which is why I said…" His honesty had taken much of the wind out of her sails. "Which is exactly why…"

"You aren't exactly the poster child for long-term commitment, either."

Molly sucked in a surprised breath. "What does that mean?"

"I checked around. Anytime a man gets remotely close to you, you dump them."

"I do not," she scoffed. "I've had serious relationships. Stop projecting your shortcomings on me."

"You've had *safe* relationships," Chandler countered. "In the past five years, you've only dated nerdy professors and boring accountant types. Safe."

"And you've only dated wispy model types with single-digit IQs who've thrown up everything they've ever eaten. So your point is what?"

"My point is," he began, standing and, gently taking her hands in order to tug her to her feet. "Maybe we're both due for a change."

"I…I don't want a change."

Chandler peered down at her, watching the pulse at the base of her throat pound. At least he wasn't alone. That was good, right? For the first time in forever, Chandler felt vulnerable. How could this dainty, albeit stubborn, little intellectual have him so off balance?

He'd built a lifetime of confidence with women,

but that all seemed to slip away as he looked down into her shimmering green eyes. He felt awkward, cautious almost. And aware. Very aware.

He stepped into her, feeling the outline of her body fit against his. Tentatively he lifted her hands until her palms rested against his chest. The fluttery feel of her fingertips was somehow more erotic than skin against skin. His body's reaction was immediate and intense.

He rested his palm against her cheek as his own need intensified. It didn't matter if they were in the middle of a hospital, he was aware of nothing save the anticipation of tasting her lips.

Chandler struggled with his own desire. Though he wanted to kiss her more than he wanted his next breath, she had to want it more.

She watched as his gaze fell to her mouth, followed almost immediately by the pad of his thumb. Her lips parted slightly as he applied pressure, rubbing his thumb across her bottom lip in an even, calculated motion that was more erotic than any kiss she'd ever received.

What had begun as a gentle action, began building, making her pulse race unevenly, carrying the sensation to the rest of her body in a series of electric shocks. The electricity pooled in her stomach, blending with the need that turned her breathing shallow.

Reflexively, her fingers gripped the soft fabric of

his shirt, balling it into tight fists as she felt herself press against him. She knew this was a bad idea. She knew it in her brain, but her body didn't much care what her mind thought. Not when she was so close to feeling the magic of his mouth covering hers.

Want had turned to need. She lurched upward, standing on tiptoe in the hopes of making contact. But he was having none of it. Even when Molly's hands moved up and grasped the back of his neck, he head didn't lower. His mouth lingered tantalizingly out of reach.

She almost cried out when he stopped touching her mouth, but then she felt his fingers lace in the back of her hair, gently tugging her backward. She was ready. More than ready. Teetering on desperate. Her body felt as if it might explode from the waiting.

"Not…just…yet."

He shifted slightly, spreading his legs so that she fit more closely against him. Any closer and she was sure she'd simply melt into him. An option that was immensely appealing.

His body was solid and warm. She felt the strained muscles of his legs against her thighs, and it threatened to make her knees buckle. "Why?" *Was that raspy, husky voice hers?*

"You have to apologize first."

"For what?"

"For doubting my motives. For criticizing my reason for coming."

"I do doubt your motives, and your reason for coming was…lame."

His lips brushed her forehead in a series of small, warm kisses that left her longing for the real thing.

"I was being nice to you, Molly. Not asking you to marry me."

"Good," she said on a rush of breath. "Because I would never marry someone like you. Or anyone for that matter."

His kisses stalled, but his mouth remained pressed against her skin. "No one? Ever?"

Tired of waiting for him, she arched her back and planted a warm, wet kiss against his neck. She felt a certain satisfaction when his body contracted and she heard a positively guttural sound rumble in his throat. His skin smelled and tasted fresh and clean.

"You're distracting me," Chandler rasped. "Intentionally, I think."

"Smart man." She punctuated each word with a warm, wet flick of her tongue.

He gripped her shoulders. Hopefully she was driving him over whatever edge he'd chosen to plant his feet. Good. There was something wonderful about this little shift in power.

He stilled her by applying pressure in the fingers bracketing her shoulders. Molly looked up just in time to see Val enter the room.

She jumped away from Chandler, but the guilty overreaction seemed lost on Val. Instead, her brow was wrinkled, and deep lines of concern seemed etched into her skin.

"Is something wrong?" Chandler asked, allowing his hands to fall to Molly's hips, where they rested comfortably.

Too comfortably perhaps.

She was about to twist away from him when Val spoke.

"There's been another explosion."

Chapter Eight

"I don't know why it went off early," he insisted. This whole scene made him feel stupid. And it reminded him of another time. He didn't like it one bit.

This should all have been over by now. But here he was, trying to explain what he didn't understand himself. They had carefully taken the bomb from the old Greeley Mine to her house. He'd done everything perfectly. It shouldn't have gone off. Not until he called the number.

"Injuring the deputy was an unfortunate mistake." He knew that. "It wasn't my fault."

The look he got in response made his shoulders slump. He knew that look. How many times had his mother given him that same disdainful look? It wasn't fair. He couldn't be responsible for a mechanical malfunction.

"They go off sometimes." He wished he hadn't given such a lame excuse as soon as he'd said it out loud.

"If you are unable to control the explosion, what *exactly* was the point of orchestrating the turn of events down to the last second? I'm very disappointed in you. Very disappointed indeed. I was counting on your ability. We needed a demonstration of your leadership for the others. How can we possibly hope to achieve our goal if you cannot be counted on to perform as planned?"

"The second bomb went off just like it was supposed to."

"True." His companion's scowl retreated. "And luckily for you, the deputy will recover."

"I wouldn't have cared if she died."

The disapproval crept back into his face and voice. "I would. As should you. Killing someone in the law enforcement community would have brought undue difficulties to us. Now is not the time to lose our focus. Not if you want success."

"Of course I do."

"I have other commitments," he said as he rose and went toward the door. "You know what to do next."

"It'll be perfect."

"Make sure that it is."

As soon as he was alone, he grabbed the ashtray off the table and flung it against the wall. It shattered and left a fist-size hole in the veneered paneling. "Dammit!" He stood, then paced the worn, dated shag carpeting that over the years had faded to the drab olive green of his mother's special-recipe pea soup. It had tasted how it had looked. Mother was no cook.

He raked his fingers through his hair, then gripped the greasy strands and yanked. "Dammit, damn—yeah! Wait a minute…."

A new idea came to him. An idea of his very own. One that would make up for the screwup with the bomb. One that would cement his destiny.

He thought it through. Well, enough to bring a smile to his face. This was it. This was how he could prove once and for all that he was the only one fit to lead. He was the only one with vision. Oh, man. His idea was *perfect*. Absolutely perfect. And brilliant. He'd show everyone.

"I LOVED THAT CAR," Chandler whined as he looked at the burned-out shell wafting thick plumes of acrid black smoke into the air in the hospital parking lot.

A small group of people had gathered, watching as the fire crew finished dousing the last of the flames. Some wore hospital scrubs, others, street clothes. They all wore shocked expressions. Understandable. This was the first car bombing for Jasper.

"Did you have insurance?" Molly inquired.

"Yes, but a car is a man's…um—?"

"Phallic symbol?"

He gave her a sidelong glance. It was hard to get

angry. Not when her hair was wild and her expression slightly bemused from their encounter.

Encounter? He felt himself frown. *Encounter* didn't describe the way she'd felt in his arms. Encounter was too neat and organized. What he'd felt in that brief time was anything *but* organized. More like wild and frenetic. And he still suffered from the lingering effects of it.

"Nice try, Madame Freud, but not everything in life is sexual."

"Sorry. Cheap shot," she agreed easily. "I was trying for levity."

"There is nothing funny about a man's car being blown to bits."

"At least it was only your car," Molly reminded him.

Chandler felt like several kinds of a fool. The poor woman's house had been blown to hell and back. A far greater loss than a car. Even a nice, shiny red one with a custom sound system and custom rims. "It was just a car."

She shot him an amused glance. "I'm sure you can get another one. Or two. Or five."

"Was that a crack about my net worth?" He frowned. "Is that something else that you're holding against me?"

"You know what they say?" she started walking toward the hospital's entrance.

He jogged to catch up. "If I tell you you have a beautiful body will you hold it against me?"

"No, I was thinking of the cliché about rich men."

"Which is?"

She paused while he held the door for her. She tilted her face to him, smiled, then said, "Get involved with a rich guy and plan on paying dearly for the privilege."

"That's harsh."

"But honest."

"Were are you going?"

"To the pay phone. I'm calling a cab."

He reached out to take her arm. "To go where?"

"Shopping and then to my office."

"Shopping? How can you want to shop after a day like today?"

She stopped and offered an exasperated look. "I don't *want* to go shopping. I have to. My toiletries got blown up, remember?"

"You can't go running off," Chandler announced.

"I'm not going to put another deputy in danger. So you can forget that."

"I agree." His remark seemed to stun her. At least it stopped her forward progress enough for him to pull her gently to the side of the corridor. He had her back against the wall, then leaned close without touching her. "I feel the same way. If I'm John's target, then I don't want innocent people caught in the crossfire."

"What do you mean 'if'? Wasn't that your car that just went up in smoke?"

"Just like your house. We're in the same boat."

"Only your boat has a roof over its head."

"We can take care of that," he said, sorry it sounded so dismissive as soon as he saw the effect register on her face. "I just meant that it isn't a problem. You can stay with me."

"Now that's a safe alternative," she sneered. "Because John won't be bothering you."

"Not at my place," he corrected. "At the ranch."

"With women and children?" she scoffed.

"Sam is taking Callie and the kids to my cousin's house. Taylor has refused to leave, but Shane has promised to use bodily force if necessary."

A smile tugged at the corners of her mouth. "That could get ugly."

"We've got a bunkhouse of well-armed men—not to mention the sheriff—ready, willing and able to keep an eye on you."

"On me? What about you?"

"I'm a big boy." He pressed closer just to bring the point home. "Besides, I can't go to work without knowing you're safe."

"You're going to work?" she repeated, her voice rising a few notches.

"Of course. I'm not going to hide from this bozo."

"Why not?" Molly countered. "Why purposefully put yourself in harm's way?"

"Because it's my job."

"I have a job, too."

He felt his mood go dark. "Not until John is caught you don't."

"When did you become my keeper?"

"When you became the target of a madman."

"THIS IS ONLY A TRIAL," she repeated, brushing debris from her purse onto the floor of the SUV Chandler had rented. "And I will see any patient who is in crisis."

"A bigger crisis than you're having right now?"

Sighing, Molly yanked on the seat belt strapping her into the vehicle. This didn't have the hallmarks of a great decision. This was an emotional, knee-jerk reaction to his bullying techniques. "My patients depend on me."

"That'll be hard to do if you get killed."

"Thanks for that."

"I'm just saying," he argued as he turned west out of town, "it's time for you to be selfish. You can't do anyone else any good if John gets to you."

She shivered at the thought. "Doesn't something about this bother you?"

"Other than the obvious?" he asked.

"John has killed two people using two different murder weapons."

"We don't know that," Chandler reasoned. "With

nothing but a torso, it's impossible to say how he killed the mother."

"It's *impossible* to say it was the mother, but a reasonable inference can be drawn."

"Okay."

Molly's brain was working at warp speed. "Most killers use a specific weapon and stick to it until something causes them to change their MO."

"Get that from watching television?"

"Don't mock me," she warned. "I got it from spending a part of my residency studying forensic psychiatry. But John is all over the place."

"Agreed. But without knowing who he is, it's hard to know why he does anything."

"He's an organized killer," Molly concluded. "Far too organized for this to be his first foray into criminal behavior."

"Or he's damned lucky."

She acknowledged that possibility with a little nod of her head. "The mother is the key," she insisted. "That's the inciting incident."

"So, we can have Seth arrest anyone who hates their mother."

She turned and regarded his handsome profile as the last rays of sunshine poured over the mountains ahead of them. Golden highlights shone in his dark hair and were reflected in the mirrored lenses of his sunglasses.

Molly wasn't fond of the sunglasses. Partly because they prevented her from reading his expression and partly because whenever he looked at her, she saw her own image staring back. It had annoyed her during their brief but productive shopping spree. Molly had selected items without regard for price. A first for her. It wasn't that she couldn't afford nice things, it was more like an exercise in personal restraint.

Well, that had gone out the window during their time at Mindy's Fashions. And she'd done all her binge shopping under the watchful, if hidden, glare of Chandler Landry. She'd seen each outfit in the mirrored lenses of his glasses but not his impression of the garments.

Silly, she now realized, since she'd never before needed an man's opinion on her attire. So why did it matter with him?

"Arresting anyone who hates their mother is a little drastic," Molly told him. "You don't sound convinced."

"The mother may be the key, but I'm thinking this is much too calculated to be anything other than personal to you."

"To me? John's been an equal-opportunity lunatic," she reminded him. "I live alone and work alone, so John had an easier time gaining access to my office and my home. Think about it."

"I am, and I'm thinking it doesn't add up."

"Sure it does." *Could you take off those damned sunglasses?* "For a reason I've not yet ascertained,

John chose to announce the murder of his mother on your show. He was cut off, so he got mad, which sparked the resulting rampage of rage. He killed my patient because it was easier than trying something at the television station."

"But there wasn't time for surveillance," Chandler argued.

"Possibly." Molly mulled that over but couldn't come up with an explanation. Yet. "Where do you live?"

"Why?"

"Where do you live?"

"I have a house in Mountaindale, why?"

It was making sense to her now. "Mountaindale is a gated community, right?"

"Uh-huh."

"John probably knew that and realized my house was far less secure, therefore easier to bomb."

She watched as he shrugged. His broad shoulders pulled against smooth fabric, allowing her a quick peek at the corded muscles of his chest and upper arms. Molly's body responded with a dull warmth in the pit of her stomach. That wasn't good. She was far too aware of him. Far too fixated on details. Like the fact that his shirt was nubby raw silk in a shade of beige that expertly set off his richly tanned skin. Or that he had the beginnings of a beard shadowing his perfectly sculpted chin. And that regardless of the harried day they'd had, he looked completely at ease seated with one wrist resting atop the steering wheel.

The sun finally dropped behind the mountains, forcing Chandler to remove his sunglasses. Too bad, he thought as he tossed them on the dash. They had been a welcome mask these past few hours. He'd kept them on since they'd left the hospital. Their mirrored finish made it impossible for her to see him staring at her. Ogling, if he was honest with himself.

"I don't think I'm the target," he said after contemplating her points. All of which, he thought to himself, were exceptional and insightful.

"It makes more sense than John being after me. You're the celebrity."

He almost cringed. He didn't much care for that aspect of his life. He thought of it as a necessary evil, especially lately. Which reminded him, he had a phone call to return. Lord, if she thought he was public now, he hated to think how she would feel if his closely guarded secret ever became public knowledge. He pushed those thoughts out of his head. No sense worrying about something that might never happen.

"Which would mean I was easier to find," he reasoned. "You were a fill-in for Gavin, which means John could not have possibly known you were going to be on the show. Which really makes no sense at all."

"Neither does that comment," she told him.

His mind whirled. "You filled in for Gavin. Last minute, right?"

"Yes."

"Who else knew you were going to do the show?"

"No one," she assured him. "I didn't agree until the last minute. Gavin had to beg me."

"Gee, thanks," he grumbled.

"Nothing personal," she insisted. "I just don't like being on television. Gavin thought it would be good for book sales."

"I'm sure it will be."

"Let's not get into a pissing contest about the use and misuse of the media," she said. "I agreed to go on your show for two reasons. One, I was helping a friend and two, I want my book to do well. You have no idea how competitive publishing can be."

"Hmm," he said noncommittally." Helping a friend? How good a friend? Don't ask, don't tell. He took a breath and went for it. "How good a friend?"

"You're the one who did a background check, you tell me."

"I'm serious." His tone was harsher than he'd intended. "I'm sorry, I was just asking because it could be important." He heard her derisive little laugh. "It could be. Aside from my producer and me, Gavin was the only other person who knew you'd be on the show."

"And Rachel," she clarified. "I wrote it into my calendar at the college. Which isn't exactly a private thing. Any number of people are in and out of the office, and the book just lies open on the desk."

"That's helpful. But you didn't actually speak to anyone?"

"Nope. But I can assure you, Gavin couldn't possibly be involved. I've known him for more than a decade."

"And you'd know if he had a screw loose?"

"He's the head of the psychiatry department, Chandler. Stop finding reasons to dislike a man you don't know just because I do."

"Who said I disliked him?" Which, by the way is juvenile, silly and dead-on. I'm a jerk. I'm jealous of a complete stranger. Bad enough. But jealous of a man who *might* have a relationship with a woman I *don't* have a relationship with is just wrong. And pathetic.

"Your tone of voice," she explained evenly. "Not that I think you deserve an explanation, but Gavin is like a father to me. He wouldn't hurt me. Just the opposite. He's done everything he can to help my career."

He had to take her proclamation at face value. For now. If not he'd look like a complete idiot, and that wasn't exactly the impression he had in mind. Not if he hoped to pick up were he'd left off.

And boy, did he hope. And hope and hope. He swallowed, banishing the lump of desire from further constricting his throat. "Okay, what about other people in your life? Men for example."

There aren't any. Nope, she couldn't admit to that. It would make her sound like a desperate spinster. Which, she concluded as she got her first glimpse of the impressive house in the distance, would only make her feel worse about herself. She'd all but ripped his clothing off at the hospital. *Worse, I licked him!* That was way too personal. And it was all happening way too fast.

"I didn't tell any of my friends—male or female— that I was doing your show. Another dead end."

The Lucky 7 Ranch was huge and impressive, much like the men who owned it. At least the ones she'd met thus far. Specifically the one pulling the SUV to a stop in the center of the horseshoe-shaped drive. The house was old but lovingly maintained. Molly was taken by the size and the workmanship.

"Impressive," she said as she climbed the first of a dozen stairs leading up to a beautifully carved double door.

Chandler was loaded down with sacks and garment bags yet still managed to take the steps two at a time without any discernable effort.

"…or I'll shoot you myself!" came the bellowing male voice as one of the front doors blew open.

Molly recognized Shane Landry from her earlier visits to the house. He was more rugged and outdoorsy than the rest of the brood. Maybe it was the long hair captured with a leather tie at the nape of his neck. Or maybe it was just the jeans and worn work shirt. Or the scowl.

It melted somewhat when he saw Molly. "Hello, Doc. Sorry we can't stay."

Taylor, all hundred or so pounds of her, was draped over the large man's shoulder, feet kicking wildly in the air.

"Put me down this instant!" Her fists pounded against Shane's solidly built back.

Molly wondered if they'd already gone a few rounds. Shane was sporting a large bruise below his left eye and another, less purple one, near his wrist. Instinctively Molly cowered against the hand-tooled railing as Shane continued, undeterred by the flailing woman in the fireman's carry.

"Molly!" Taylor called, her blue eyes brilliant with anger, "Tell this *buffoon* to put me down."

"Seth said to take her into town. At least until they catch your stalker."

"H-he's got a point," Molly called to her friend. "It really isn't safe to be around us with Chandler's stalker still out there."

"I can shoot better than he can," Taylor announced as Shane swung her down.

He held her at the waist as he fumbled in his pocket. "Where are my keys?" he demanded of no one in particular. "If I don't find my key in a few seconds—"

"Take the rental," Chandler called, tossing the keys to his brother. "Taylor, cooperate. I've never asked you to do anything, but I'm asking you to do this."

Taylor stopped struggling but didn't ease up at all on the killer glare she had fixed on the youngest Landry. "Don't guilt me," she pleaded, pouting.

"I look like an assault victim," Shane groused, pulling up his sleeve to assess the damage.

"You bruise easier than ripe fruit," Taylor taunted. "If I'm being banned from my own house, then get a move on. You've got to get back here inside an hour so you can get the roast out of the oven."

"I can do that," Molly offered.

"And it isn't your house," Shane said as he deposited Taylor inside the car. "It's my house. You're an employee. A fact you seem to forget. You really should learn your place, woman."

"How about I kick you in *your* place?" Taylor returned, eyes flashing.

Chandler was chuckling as he led Molly inside. She failed to see the humor. "Are they always so physical?"

He nodded. "Taylor fits right in here."

"Should I have bought body armor?"

His laughter filled the elegant foyer. She marveled at the beautiful molding and highly polished paneling. The home had a decidedly masculine feel to it—understandable. Yet the smell of the food mingling with the faint scent of baby powder gave the place a homey feel that welcomed her inside.

She followed Chandler up to the second floor. It was a tribute to the nineteenth century. Small tables lined the long corridor, each illuminated by a period lamp casting a warm glow to mark the way. The smell of lemon oil hung in the air, mingling with the other aromas. Chandler stopped just beyond an open door, tossing his head to indicate she should follow inside.

It wasn't at all what she'd expected. It was a frilly room. It had to be a guest room. She couldn't imagine any of the Landry men choosing or tolerating white eyelet and doilies. Her surprise was forgotten as soon as she saw the view.

A nearly full moon hung low in the sky, just above the majestic peaks in the distance. Though it was summer, snow painted the very tops of the mountains, allowing them to glisten and reflect the moonlight.

"It looks like a postcard," she murmured appreciatively as she gazed outside. Many outbuildings dotted the landscape along with a couple of corrals and miles and miles of fencing.

"My grandfather chose well," he said, coming to her side after depositing her things. "Every room in the house has a great view." His fingers splayed at the small of her back as his thumb hooked her waist. "Move over here," he said, his voice close to her ear.

If he kept his hands on her and continued to speak in that low, inviting tone, she'd probably move into the fires of hell if he asked.

He bent down and pointed out to the right. "Look over there, you can see five lakes from up here."

She did and she could. It was truly beautiful.

And interrupted by the annoying chirp of his cell phone. "Landry."

She continued to enjoy the view until she felt his fingers tense against her spine.

"Out of the question," he barked into the phone. Then a pause, then, "Well, think of something else."

"What?" she whispered, sensing his agitation.

He shook his head. "Dr. Jameson isn't doing that. I won't—"

"What?" she demanded, grabbing the telephone and jerking it away from his ear. "Who is that and what won't I do?"

"It's Mike."

The name didn't register.

"My producer?" he prodded. "He wants you on air tonight."

She heard a garbled male voice shouting on the other end of the phone. Her eyes locked on Chandler and she tugged for sole possession of the cell phone. After a brief standoff, he relinquished it to her.

"This is Dr. Jameson."

"Mike Murray, Dr. Jameson. We have a situation here."

"Which is?"

"John is threatening to blow the station if you don't appear on the eleven-o'clock news. He also said he'd kill another one of your patients if you don't—"

"He threatened my patie—"

Chandler bent his head and wrestled the phone so they now shared it. "Get the bomb squad to handle it," he said.

"I've done that. They've called the dog handlers but they're coming from Park City so they might not make it here in enough time."

"That's their problem," Chandler insisted.

"I know this isn't good. We can do a remote," Mike suggested. "I'm not trying to put anyone in undue danger, but I'm between a rock and a hard place here. I can't risk having this lunatic blow up the whole station. We can figure something out."

"I'll do it," Molly called, ignoring Chandler's harsh, disapproving look. "Figure out some location that isn't readily recognizable. I'll be there."

"I know I'm asking a lot of you, Doctor."

"You're going to get her killed!" Chandler insisted.

"Or I can do nothing," Molly reasoned, "and he might kill another innocent person. I don't want that to happen."

"There has to be a better option," Chandler said.

"Well—" she paused and took a fortifying breath

"—until someone comes up with one, let's do everything possible to do what John wants without anyone getting killed."

"I don't like this, Molly."

"I'm not too thrilled, either," she admitted. "But I don't have a choice.

"Work out a location for a remote," he said into the receiver, then flipped the phone closed.

He reached out and allowed his fingertip to trace the line of her jaw. The look in his eyes increased her pulse tenfold. "I've got a bad feeling about this."

She reached up and covered his hand with hers. "This—the remote broadcast. Or this—me?"

Her breath caught as he dipped his head toward hers.

Chapter Nine

Chandler's mouth hovered above her as he whispered, "I look at you and I can't think of anything but this."

He slid one hand up her back, and cradled her face in his other palm. Using his thumb, Chandler tilted her head back and hesitated only fractionally before his mouth found hers. Instinctively Molly's hands went to his waist. She could feel the tapered muscles stiffen in response to her touch.

The scent of soap and cologne filled her nostrils as the exquisite pressure of his mouth increased. His fingers began to slowly massage their way toward her spine. Until the tips began a sensual counting of each vertebra. His other hand held her face exactly where he wanted it—heaven help her—where they both wanted it. Beneath his mouth.

Her mind was no longer capable of rational thought. All her attention was on the intense sensations filling her with fierce desire.

Heart racing in her ears, she allowed herself to

revel in the feel of his strong body pressing her against the wall. It was so annoyingly macho, but she loved feeling the weight of him, the strength of his desire, the heat of his maleness against her. He deepened the kiss into something more demanding, and she succumbed to a potent dose of longing.

Molly slid her hands from his trim waist up his back, feeling the flex and play of his muscles beneath his shirt. She began to explore the solid contours of his body beneath the soft, silk fabric. It was like touching the smooth, sculpted surface of a granite statue. Everywhere she touched she felt the distinct outline of corded muscle. She could even feel the vibration of his erratic breathing.

When he lifted his head, she had to fight to keep from giving in to her strong urge to pull him back to her. His eyes met and held hers as he quietly looked down, searching her face. His breath came in short, almost raspy gulps and she watched the tiny vein at his temple race in time with her own rapid heartbeat.

"Second thoughts?" she asked, almost afraid of his reply.

"I don't want us to think, Molly. Not right now."

"That isn't very responsible behavior," she said.

"Who says we have to be responsible when our lives have been upended?" he countered as his thumb hooked under her chin.

She tried to ignore the sudden tightness in the pit

of her stomach. But she knew she couldn't ignore the blatant invitation in his devastating gaze. "That's the best possible reason for us to take a step back and not act on a physical attraction."

"I disagree." He leaned in to brush his mouth ever so lightly against hers. "But it's nice to know you're physically attracted."

She thought about denying it. Then she realized she didn't want to. Not here. Not now.

She tilted up her face, using her palms on his back to draw him closer. "Kiss me like you mean it," she whispered playfully against his lips.

Chandler's head dipped, blocking out their surroundings. Her mouth opened beneath his, and she tasted his desire. Bubbles of her own need shimmered through her. It had been a long time since she'd taken something purely for herself, while damning the consequences.

But kissing Chandler Landry like this was nothing like buying a pair of ridiculously expensive shoes just because she liked the color. A pair of fuchsia heels didn't make her lose all rational thought, a good pair of shoes didn't make her blood sing.

His tongue played with hers, darting and teasing, until Molly stood on tiptoe, crushing her mouth up to his and using her own tongue to tango with his in a dance as old as time.

And all the while his thumb stroked her cheek in

slow counterpoint to the churning cauldron the kiss was igniting inside her. Molly found herself with handfuls of his shirt gripped in her fist at the small of his back as the kiss went on and on and on.

And it would have gone further. She needed it to—wanted it to.

But *he* didn't.

That fact took several minutes to wade through the thick, sexually-charged fog of her brain. Once it registered, she felt a torrent of emotions rain down on her like a violent, disorganized storm. His hands—the same wonderful hands that she longed to give free rein of her body—were now holding her shoulders, setting her back and away from him.

She was angry. Frustrated. Disappointed. And thoroughly embarrassed. *When did I become Suzy Slut?* she wondered as her fingers went reflexively to her mouth, feeling the last vestiges of his kiss fade away.

"I don't know what got into me," she said, hoping her tone was light. "I guess the stress of the last few days coupled with—"

Chandler's forefinger crooked under her chin, lifting her face toward his. She could easily lose herself in the brilliant depths of chocolate brown. Especially when she read the lingering passion in his gaze punctuated by the uneven way his breath spilled from his lips.

"It wasn't stress, Molly."

She wiggled away from his touch, not completely trusting herself quite yet. In fact, it was completely possible that she might throw self-respect to the wind, tackle him to the ground and have her way with him.

She groaned inwardly. *Have my way with him? When did I start thinking like an Amish virgin?* Maybe she'd been a little closer to that explosion than she'd thought. That was a possible explanation.

"Stress brings out—" She stopped in midthought, irritated by his breathtaking, self-satisfied, skeptical smile.

Chandler shifted to lean against the wall, his intense eyes still fixed on her face. He reached out to brush a few strands of hair from her face and Molly struggled to keep from reacting to his touch.

"I kissed you because I've wanted to since I saw you walk into the studio."

"Doing something just because you want to is a little boy's rationalization," she said. "You kissed me for the same reason I kissed you back. One or both of us might die tonight, so it was a simple satisfaction of the normal sexual curiosity between a man and a woman."

He whistled and shook his dark head. "That's one possibility."

"You disagree?"

"Nope. I would just have simplified it."

She frowned. "That was a simple and concise explanation."

His fingertip stroked the side of her face, moving down until his hand rested against just above her collarbone. He leaned forward, his warm breath teasing her ear as he said, "No, Molly. The simple truth is, I want you. Kissing is a good start down that path."

SHE WASN'T SURE what bothered her most. Knowing that the microphone being clipped to her blouse was for the benefit of a murderous lunatic or replaying Chandler's words in her head.

I want you.

She needed to focus. She took a long swallow of the tepid coffee she'd been handed by one of the five crew people setting up the remote broadcast.

She was seated in a metal folding chair, allowing a youngish woman to clip the microphone pack to the waistband of her new sage-colored slacks. Normally Molly enjoyed new-outfit moments. Very few things were as personally uplifting as being decked out, head to toe, in new stuff. Since the new stuff was only a result of having all her other stuff blown to bits, the experience didn't have the usual fun attached to it.

Her stomach rumbled, then knotted when she spotted Chandler huddled in the corner of the makeshift studio with his producer. It didn't seem fair that the mere sight of him should inspire such strong longings deep inside her.

Sure it does. I'm totally hot for the guy.

She was acting like a foolish teenager lusting after the most popular guy in school, all the while knowing full well he would break her heart in the end. *My heart?* She swallowed more coffee, hoping the caffeine might restore order to her thoughts.

First off, she didn't fall for a man she'd known for a little more than forty-eight hours. That was, she added kindly, for hopeless romantics or—less kindly—complete morons. Secondly, Chandler was out of her league. A stable, responsible, mature woman, which she was, didn't set her sights on a man like him. He was…

Funny and compassionate?

A rich womanizer who lived in the public eye.

Kind and caring?

Who knew, probably from birth, what buttons to push to make a woman melt into a quivering pile of hormonal need.

Genuinely concerned for my safety and well-being?

Okay, so she didn't have an objection for that one, but it was out there. She knew it. Under than devastatingly handsome exterior lay the wrong kind of man for her.

When did I get a "kind"? she wondered, annoyed.

Flanked by his producer, Mike, Chandler walked over to Molly. He hadn't been this keyed-up before a shoot since his first live shot from the Iraqi desert. And it didn't help that Molly looked as if she was about to be tossed to the lions.

"How are you holding up?"

She shrugged. "Okay. Where exactly are we, though?"

He offered an apologetic smile. "It's our warehouse. Mike had them move out the old equipment stored here, and voilà, Studio B is born."

"So, what's the plan?"

Chandler took the cup of coffee from her grasp, deposited it on the floor, then reached for her hand. "The station has been running a promo about your appearance on the eleven-o'clock edition. Your segment will start about seventeen minutes into the broadcast."

She blinked up at him. "You're doing the newscast?"

Pulling her to her feet, he gave her hand a little squeeze. "It's my job, Molly. Besides, we all agree that since John has already blown up my car, involving another newscaster at this point could add another target to John's hit list."

Her hand stiffened in his for a minute before she said, "I hadn't thought about that."

"We did," Mike added as he came up beside her. "If you'll come with me?"

Molly dropped Chandler's hand and followed the producer over to stand behind one of the bulky, robotic cameras aimed at the makeshift set. Chandler slipped on a dark-chocolate-colored jacket, adjusted his tie and clipped his mike into place.

A curved desk had been carried in, along with two chairs and a large plywood wall covered in a blue fabric. "What's that for?" Molly inquired as Chandler sat down.

"Chromakey canvass," Mike explained. "The computer back at the control booth can superimpose images behind Chandler. Television magic," Mike said with a wink before slipping a headset on.

Having nothing to do, Molly stood back and watched as Chandler made it look effortless. Her palms were sweaty just thinking about going back on camera. He was relaxed, affable, and she was sure that the viewing audience had no idea of what was actually happening behind the scenes.

"...had a small problem on our regular set. Thanks to a lot of hard work by the people behind the scenes here at WMON, we're going a little low-tech tonight," Chandler announced. "Our news begins tonight with a sad story on the international front."

Molly listened to the news, halfheartedly processing the events of the day as her own nervousness ebbed and flowed. She knew there were three deputies and two state police cars guarding their location, so she was pretty confident that John wouldn't be able to do anything while they were on air. But there was still the problem of her camera aversion. The alternative wasn't an option. John had made that very clear. If she didn't go on, he would kill some innocent person, and Molly simply couldn't live with that. She was having a hard time processing Mrs. Zarnowski's death. She certainly didn't want to be responsible for harm coming to anyone else on her account.

At the prescribed time, she took the seat next to Chandler.

"You okay?"

"Peachy," she insisted, wiping her palms on a tissue. "What do we do if John doesn't call in?"

"Nothing," he assured her as he reached up to straighten her collar. "He might not. He said he just wanted to see you."

"That has a very high creepy factor," she muttered.

"We're back in ten!" Mike called from his half-hidden post behind the camera.

Molly laced her fingers and rested her clasped hands on the desk in front of her, then plastered a deceptively calm expression on her face.

"In five!"

"Ready?"

"Yep."

"Three…two!" Mike's hand went down at the same instant the green light above the camera lighted.

"We're back with Dr. Molly Jameson, author of *The Relationship Mambo,*" Chandler said. "Welcome back, Doctor."

"Thank you." She was glad that her voice didn't betray the anxiety that had all but paralyzed her. Her throat was dry, leaving the stale taste of coffee pasted onto her tongue.

By the miracle of technology, telephone calls were forwarded from the station's phone bank to the warehouse and finally to a speaker placed just off camera and operated by one of the crew. "You're on with Dr. Jameson," Chandler greeted.

She braced, fully expecting to hear John's voice echo through the room. Instead, she found herself listening to the trials and tribulations of a teenage girl who'd been grounded for six months and wanted advice on how to regain her parent's trust.

"You have to earn it back," Molly responded. "Start small, Crystal. Demonstrate to your parents that you understand what you did was wrong and then accept your responsibility in this punishment."

"But all I did was break curfew!" the girl whined.

"By how much?" Molly asked.

"Just a couple of hours."

"Have you thought about what your parents were going through for those two hours?"

"I knew they'd be mad," the girl admitted, "but their punishment is totally way harsh. I mean, there was this really cool party and everyone else stayed so it wasn't fair for me to have to leave at midnight. I'm fifteen, midnight is way too young for someone my age. That's, like, a junior-high curfew."

"That's a separate issue," Molly told the girl gently. "You have to take responsibility for your actions. You made a choice to defy the limitations imposed by your parents. In making that choice, you also have to accept the consequences of making your parents worry."

"They say they love me, but, like, how can you totally punish someone you love?"

"Punishment is a way of showing love," Molly counseled. "Your parents have a responsibility to provide you guidance. That's their job. I'm very sure that they don't like this situation either, but by punishing you, they are teaching you to respect the limitations they have imposed. Believe it or not, life will always have limits," Molly told the girl. "Your parents are simply preparing you for the real world. If they didn't love you, they wouldn't care what you do."

Mike began jumping up and down, waving his chubby arms back and forth excitedly. It caused Molly to lose her train of thought for a second.

"D-does that help you?" she asked.

"I wanted to know how to bail on restriction," the girl grunted. "Not get another lecture."

"Thanks for calling," Chandler interrupted. "Dr. Jameson, we have John on the line."

Molly's heart rate spiked. "Y-yes, John?"

"Interesting advice, Doctor," he sneered.

Molly heard the venom in his tone all the way down to her toes. This was one angry guy. "Let's not discuss the previous caller, John. Tell me about yourself."

"I'm a Leo and I like long walks on the beach."

She saw the muscles in Chandler's jaw tense out of the corner of her eye.

"Do you have a question, John?"

"Yea. I want to know how it feels to know you're gonna die soon."

Chapter Ten

"That went well," Molly said as she and Chandler walked out into the cool evening air. The scent of exhaust from the idling trucks nearby left a metallic taste in her mouth as she followed Chandler to the SUV under the watchful eyes of the law enforcement officers scattered around the lot.

"It did," he agreed as he held the door for her, taking her hand as she made the climb up into the vehicle. "John saw you on television. Hopefully that will keep him from hurting anyone for a while."

Molly hoped so, too, though John's cryptic question still careened around in her mind. What had she ever done to bring the wrath of a sociopath raining down on her head? It simply didn't make sense.

"You're quiet," Chandler said as he steered out onto the highway west of town.

"Thinking," she murmured, adjusting her seat belt. "Or trying to, at least. I'm a little sleep deprived right now."

His hand suddenly rested on her knee. It was comforting and exciting all at once. And she was simply too exhausted to sort through the many reasons why she should avoid repeating the earlier mistake of kissing him. Wanting to kiss him, actually. That was what bothered her so much. The consuming, thrilling want that his mere presence inspired.

"I know you need to get to bed, but I've got to stop by my place to pack a few things. Okay?"

"Sure."

The drive out to Mountaindale Estates took less than fifteen minutes. In that time, Molly had suffered no fewer than three nap jerks. The hum of the car's engine, her fatigue and the comfort of knowing that she wasn't alone had allowed her to relax to the point where she would slip into a near-sleep state, then her body would convulse back to consciousness.

Chandler used a small black remote to activate the iron gate to the community. It swung open regally. Though it was nearing midnight, the full moon and decorative streetlamps allowed her to see many of the lovely homes set back from the street. It was a newer development, complete with manicured laws, sculpted hedges and trees standing at precise increments along the curb like soldiers at attention.

They had passed maybe a dozen homes when he

turned into a long drive. The instant they approached, floodlights illuminated the curved, slightly sloping drive and the impressive front of his house.

"I wouldn't have pictured this," she commented when he parked and cut the engine. "This is so different from your family's ranch."

"That was the point," he said, leading the way to the front door. "I wanted something more personal to me. And neat."

So he liked modern architecture, she mused. The house was an odd blend of glass, wood, steel and concrete. Stepping across the threshold, she was surprised to smell orange.

"My cleaning woman was here today," he explained.

She probably would have spent more time wondering how he had read her mind, but she was too taken with the house to speak. As he walked ahead of her, flipping switches, her eyes darted from one wonderful feature to the next. The foyer and living room had art glass light fixtures in soft blues. As she ventured further, she found a state-of-the-art chrome and stainless steel kitchen dominated by a warm butcher-block island. Above the island, chrome lamps dangled from the high ceiling, flooding the area with the perfect amount of light for the workspace. The cabinets were glass, trimmed in light wood that matched the flooring.

The kitchen opened into a large dining area, complete with a shared counter that would be perfect as a breakfast bar or a buffet server.

"Impressive," she commented, her gaze drawn to the large oils hanging in the dining room. The lush landscapes provided color in the otherwise sparsely decorated area.

"The paintings?" he asked, tossing his keys on the counter.

"Everything," she gushed easily. "This is my dream house," she admitted as she ran her fingers over the ceramic tiles behind the double sink. The artwork was amazing, and she'd bet her last dollar they were all originals.

"Callie painted those for me last Christmas. And Savannah found the glass and ceramic stuff. It helps to have willing sisters-in-law when you're fixing a place up. Make yourself at home," he added as he headed toward the floating staircase of wood plank and wrought iron. "I won't be long."

Zombielike, Molly roamed around the first floor, admiring each room and its unique contents. She could hear him upstairs, and though she longed to see what gems were on the upper floor, she didn't dare follow him up there. Not when there was sure to be a bed close by.

She contented herself by strolling back through the living room, past the cream-colored leather sofas, down the hallway. Moonlight poured in from arched glass above expertly appointed window treatments. There was a powder room that also contained some lovely ceramic tile work along with the necessities. And again, the art glass light fixtures with a hint of color were a subtle and perfect complement to the decor.

She peeked around an open door, after turning on the switch, and discovered a neatly appointed home office. She had to smile, it was neat as a pin and organized better than a card catalog. She remembered his office at the television station, so it should have come as no surprise that Chandler's home would be equally well arranged.

There wasn't a single fingerprint or streak on the massive glass-topped desk that dominated the room. A large, black leather chair was centered behind the desk and a laptop computer was centered in front of that.

Even his pile of colored sticky notes was stacked as if shrink-wrapped, and three containers were evenly spaced beside the notes. One for pens, one for pencils, and the last held markers and highlighters. Very neat.

"Very anal," she chuckled. Then she spotted the books. Well, four books in particular. L S. Connor books to be exact. He had her dream house and read her favorite author. "Amazing."

Then on closer inspection, she rethought that notion. Though she didn't remove them from their assigned places—mainly because she was afraid to mess with his OCD tendencies—she could tell the books were unread. The dust jackets were crisp and the pages seemed too pristine to have been touched by human hands. Her copies were mangled, spotted with water and well loved. And, she concluded, since the books had been relegated to a lonely, lower shelf all by themselves, she assumed the books were gifts he'd been too kind to refuse.

She guessed one of the sisters-in-law might be the culprit. L. S. Connor was a wildly popular author, especially with women, and it made perfect sense that one of the women in his life would discover the appeal of the Wyatt adventures and need to share.

Before leaving the room she made a mental note to ask him about the books. Encourage him to read them. She turned and fell against him.

She was startled and aware. Too aware. Even though she'd taken a reflexive step backward, and the only part of him touching her was his steadying hands at her waist, Molly felt the familiar sensation of heat surging through her body.

"Sorry," she mumbled.

"I'm not," he teased. "Feel free to run into me anytime."

She shrugged out of his grasp. Tilting her head back, she met and held his gaze. "Let's set some rules, Landry."

"We need rules?"

She sucked in a breath and let it out slowly. "I do."

"Shoot."

He seemed entirely too reasonable. Or maybe she was just a taut wire of raw emotion and envious at the ease with which he seemed to handle everything. "You have to be strong for both of us."

His brow wrinkled into an amused frown. "I've been the picture of restraint. Even though I'd like nothing more than to carry you upstairs and—"

She held her hand up to stop him. "That's the point. That's why we need rules. Look, I'm a wreck, and the easiest thing in the world would be to jump into bed with you."

He reached for her. "Glad we're in agreement. I like how you think."

She sidestepped his grip. "I said it would be the *easiest* thing. Not the *best* thing."

"Speak for yourself."

Damn him. His slightly cocked head and easy smile were making this very difficult. "Look, I think you've been a real stand-up guy these past days."

"Why do I feel like I'm about to be dumped?"

"Like that's ever happened to you," she scoffed.

He leaned against the doorjamb. "It has. Several times in fact." He paused and made a production out of stroking his chin. "But I was assured in all those instances that it wasn't me, it was them."

Molly bit back a laugh. She'd used that line a time or two. "Whatever. My point is, I'm totally needy right now, which means my defenses are completely shredded, which means I probably might be dumb enough to sleep with you purely as a diversion and that's not a good enough reason."

"I agree."

She blinked. "So, you'll back off?"

"A little. For a while."

No harsh look, no recrimination in his tone. Total, easy acceptance. She didn't know whether to be happy that he'd acquiesced so easily or affronted for the very same reason. "Okay, then. We're fine?"

"Moderately fine," he answered as he motioned for her to head out of the room.

"So this is going to be an issue for you?"

"It's an issue for me," he admitted when they reached the front door. He placed his hand on the knob, then turned and met her gaze. "I want you, Molly. That's my problem. I haven't made any secret of that, but I'm a big boy, I can handle it. I'll wait."

"Thank you." She started out into the night.

Chandler leaned down and added, "For a while."

And as he got back into the SUV, he hoped the time would pass quickly. He hoped it would but had his doubts. He ached.

His cell phone rang as he was leaving the development. "Landry."

"Make that Landry*s*," Chance gleefully yelped over the line. "Val and I are on the way to the hospital now."

"Congrats, bro," he said, feeling thrilled and anxious at the news. "How long?"

"I'm a doctor, not a psychic," Chance replied dryly. "The baby will come on its own time."

"It better be soon!" Val called in the distance, followed by a very loud, very primal scream. "This hurts!"

"Better go," Chance said on a rush. "If I don't get her an epidural soon, she'll probably kill me."

"Sounds like a plan. Keep me in the loop. I'll be at the ranch." He disconnected the call and told Molly what was happening.

"You should be with your family," Molly told him.

Her tone was so earnest it touched his heart. Then his brain realized that his heart had been touched and it scared the hell out of him. His heart wasn't usually one of his first body parts to be attracted to a woman.

Banishing the troubling thought from his head, he said, "Believe me, I *don't* want to be there. I'm the uncle. I get to skip the tough moments and proceed directly to the spoiling and cooing stage."

"That does have its advantages," she agreed. "Still, I don't want to keep you from a family obligation."

"Obligation?" She made it sound like a vile curse. "My family can be annoying as hell, but I never think of them as an obligation."

"You're lucky."

His interest was piqued. "Not into family?"

It was dark, but he was pretty sure she shrugged. "Not an option for me. I'm an only child and my parents are both dead."

"No aunts, uncles, cousins? No one?" He couldn't imagine that life. He didn't want to try.

"Just me," she answered in a bland, emotionless tone.

"That sucks."

"Depends on your perspective. I never had to share my toys. I had a bedroom and a bathroom to myself."

"No one to play with. No one to share your secrets with. And no one to fight with."

"I shared my secrets with girlfriends from time to time and as for the fighting, well, I have always treated that as something to avoid."

"Then you've never had a great fight. Clears the air."

"Barbaric. People should be able to sit down and rationally discuss their differences."

Chandler tossed his head back and laughed. "Believe me, if you're a Landry, you act first and talk later. Survival 101."

"Whatever works for you."

He rubbed the back of his neck, massaging the fatigue that had set in there. "Did you become a shrink because of your unhappy childhood?"

"I don't remember telling you that I had an unhappy childhood."

Nope, but the frost in her tone did. "Did you?"

"I became a psychiatrist because—"

"No," he cut her off gently. "Did you have an unhappy childhood?"

"No more or less than most people."

He sighed heavily. "See, Molly, this is me asking you questions so we can get to know each other better. We're building a friendship. Finding things out about each other."

"You're just trying to find a way to separate me from my panties."

"That, too," he admitted freely, "but for now I'll settle for a complete history."

"Not much to tell."

He doubted that.

"My mother died when I was thirteen. My father died when I was an undergraduate."

"Thirteen?" he repeated, his mind switching gears.

"Yes. A difficult age to lose a parent, but I got through it."

"Who knows that fact about you?"

"No one."

"No one?"

She sighed. "My girlfriend, Claire. And anyone

else who searched through obituaries. It isn't something you can keep a secret."

"Would this Claire person have told anyone?"

"Her husband. Maybe. If it came up."

"What about other people?"

"Why?"

"Maybe that's the thirteen John was hinting at when he branded the torso and stabbed your patient."

"Very improbable. Besides, as I said, my mother's death is a matter of public record."

"Here?"

"No, back east. But anyone who cared could probably get the information off the Internet. Interesting, though. I'd almost forgotten about the thirteen."

He gripped the steering wheel tighter. There was something evasive about her answer. He didn't know what, he just knew there was something guarded in her voice. "I haven't forgotten. I'm still wondering how you remembered the atomic number for aluminum."

"Free association. I also happen to know that a firing squad has thirteen members. And there were thirteen people present at the Last Supper."

"You're a regular trivia whiz."

"It's a gift."

He was glad to hear her tone return to normal. "Were you one of those people who sailed through school?"

"As if it was the last leg of the America's Cup and all my competitors sank on the first day."

"Modest," he teased. "You're lucky. I had to work for every credit."

"People tend to appreciate the things they have to work the hardest to attain."

"So what do you appreciate?"

"Life."

"Too general."

He heard her breathing and smelled the floral hint of her perfume. He was doing his best to be a gentleman, but as expected, his thoughts turned to his baser needs. He couldn't help it. She was just too appealing, and he wanted her more than he'd wanted anything in his life.

"It's the middle of the night, Chandler. Can't you interview me tomorrow?"

"It wasn't an interview."

"Felt like one," she countered. "It's what you do. You can't help yourself."

Denying all the passions simmering inside of him had a predictable effect. Chandler's mood grew dark. The SUV felt like a cage and he was the animal. Being close enough to touch her but denied the pleasure was the stick poking through the bars. Twenty-two hours without sleep wasn't helping, either. He would have loved to punch something. Anything. The frustration was getting on his last nerve.

AND IT WASN'T ANY BETTER a few hours later when he joined Shane in the kitchen. The inviting smell of coffee had roused him from a fitful sleep.

"Morning," Shane greeted from behind the paper.

He took one look at his youngest brother and felt a scowl come to his lips. "Go put some clothes on."

Shane lowered the paper and smiled. "I did. I put on my boxers."

The teasing didn't do much to improve Chandler's mood. "You jerk. I don't want Molly getting up to find your practically naked butt in the chair." He rolled the section of newspaper closest to him and smacked Shane on the top of the head. Not hard, but with enough force to let him know he was serious.

"Ouch." His brother stood and walked out of the kitchen, then returned a second later with his jeans and a shirt hooked on his index finger. His smile was broad and annoying. "I stripped these off when I heard you get up. I was just having some fun with you."

Chandler poured himself a mug of steaming coffee and then glared at Shane. "We should have put you up for adoption."

"Wasn't up to you," Shane countered affably. "Besides, the folks always loved me best."

He snorted, then sucked down another gulp in hopes that the caffeine might kick in faster. "No one loved you, Shane. We just kept you around to do chores."

"Kiss my—"

The phone rang, cutting off one of Shane's favorite directives. Both men dove for it. Shane got there first.

"Uncle Shane at your service."

Chandler was waiting for the news about Val's delivery. He was concerned about his sister-in-law's well-being, but he also knew he had picked "labor lasting less than twelve hours" in the family betting pool. But when Shane's expression grew suddenly serious, Chandler felt panic knot in his gut. They'd already had one difficult birth in the family that had, luckily, turned out okay, but he said a prayer there wasn't a second complication.

Holding the receiver out, Shane simply said, "It's Seth."

Grabbing the phone and putting it to his ear, Chandler asked, "What's up?"

"I need to speak to your house guest."

There was something ominous in Seth's tone and rather abrupt delivery. His brother was usually more laid-back. "What is it?"

"I need to talk to her Chandler. She's been keeping a pretty big secret."

Chapter Eleven

"You didn't think this was important?" Chandler's voice startled her awake. He stood beside her bed, feet braced, hands balled to fists at his side. He was so angry, Molly almost expected to see steam rising from his ears.

"Wh-what?" she asked, struggling to sit up while still three-quarters asleep.

"Jonas Black?"

She shook off the last vestiges of sleep as the name settled into the pit of her stomach like a bad taco. "Jonas? What does he have to do with this?"

"You have a restraining order against the guy, and you didn't think to mention it?"

His nostrils flared and the muscles at his jaw twitched like a strobe warning. As if she needed any warning. In anger, his eyes grew narrow and darker—black almost. And pretty darned intense.

She found it interesting, in a purely clinical way,

that she didn't find Chandler Landry in a temper the least bit terrifying. Exciting. Yes. Scary. No.

Standing, she put on her robe. "Don't burst in here yelling at me like I'm some errant child." She pivoted away on her bare feet. "I'll brush my hair and my teeth and join you downstairs in a few minutes."

She slipped inside the bathroom before he could argue. Good thing, too, because her bravado was all show. She about fell against the door, willing her heart to stop racing.

After rubbing her face, she stared at her reflection, then asked, "And you didn't say anything because?"

Because it was forever ago and no big deal. So why hadn't she told Seth or Chandler?

Molly turned on the faucet and took as much time as possible preparing for battle. And if Chandler's demeanor was any indication, it wasn't going to be pretty.

CHANDLER PACED THE FAMILY ROOM, raking his hands through his hair each time he turned to change direction. He was furious. And the knowledge that she'd been dallying for the better part of forty-five minutes didn't help much.

After speaking to Seth, he'd cursed a blue streak at Shane, only because he was handy, and then gone in search of Molly. He'd been half tempted to grab her by the ankles and yank her out of bed. Then he caught sight of her and he was just tempted.

He played the memory in his mind. The way her hair fanned out against the pillow, the flawless, pale skin shimmering in the first light of a new day. It had been a sight. Enough to stop him midstride and leave him breathless just from looking.

His inability to breathe might have been due—in large measure—to her attire. Or lack thereof. The comforter had slipped down to her waist, allowing him to see her beautiful body clad in a flimsy, lacey wisp of fabric that left nothing and everything to his imagination.

She'd been on her side, tucked into a neat position with her legs slightly bent at the knees. He knew because the small blanket didn't cover anything from about midthigh down. Though she was a small woman, he knew she was perfectly proportioned. Those legs of hers were something. Fit but not muscular and complete with a tiny mole near one ankle that he fantasized about kissing for a long, long time.

Not trusting himself, he'd gone to Taylor's room and confiscated a robe, then returned and tossed it at Molly's head. In the seconds it had taken her to sit, then stand, then pull on the garment, he'd been treated to an incredible view of scantily clad, firm, rounded breasts and slender hips. He'd actually only noticed her hips because of the single rope of pale-pink satin that she passed off as panties. And he was fairly sure that had she turned around, very little of that cute, tight butt would have been covered.

His groin tightened as he shook his head. No amount of shaking would erase that image from his mind. Nope. Every detail was stored and cataloged. He could imagine looping his fingers underneath each silky strap of her camisole, peeling it off her skin slowly until it fell to the floor, pooling on top of her pink-painted toenails. He'd repeat the action with the panties, deliberately exercising patience in removing the last barrier. Then he'd stand back and stare. Stare until he memorized every inch of her perfect body.

Who was he kidding? He wanted her so badly that if and when he did get her naked, he'd be lucky to last a minute.

Knowing that didn't improve his mood at all. She made him wait another five minutes before he heard her footfalls on the stairs. Chandler moved out into the hallway, watching her descend.

The time hadn't been wasted. She was beautiful. Though he had a secret affinity for her undergarments, he had to admit, the woman dressed well. Her chino slacks rode low on her hips, teasing him with the promise that if she moved in the right way, he'd actually get a peek of her flat, toned tummy. But she wasn't the type to flash skin. So, she'd paired the casual slacks with two tops. One was a paler version of the brilliant green of her eyes. It was one of those tank-styled things—shape-hugging with tiny straps. He couldn't actually see cleavage.

More like a subtle shadow just at the edge of the shirt that mocked him into needing to see what was beneath.

The overshirt was short-sleeved and transparent. The pattern had something to do with flowers and the overall look was utterly, annoyingly feminine. She'd applied a soft pink gloss to her lips—which were slightly parted as she reached the last step.

He led her into the family room, trying not to suck in the gloriously clean, refreshing scent of her cologne mingling with soap. Taking her by the elbow, he ignored the smooth softness of her skin—or tried to—and deposited her on the overstuffed couch, then sat beside her.

He was intentionally crowding her. Molly knew the tactic and wasn't impressed by it. Then again, he apparently hadn't been distracted by her. That little plan had backfired. Big-time. The pairing of the slacks and the shirt had been a deliberate attempt to change his focus. She'd gone to special trouble to apply makeup *and* left her hair loose hoping beyond hope that he'd forget some of his annoyance.

One look in those dark, brooding eyes told her she'd been completely unsuccessful. Miserably so. His eyes flashed with anger. His jaw was set so firmly that his dimples seemed deeper, more pronounced. And his mouth, the one that had come to her in her dreams, was drawn into a tight line.

"You aren't going to hit me or anything, right?"

He was visibly surprised, at least she guessed as much by the shock registering in his piercing gaze. "Hit you? Why would you think that?"

"You're angry. Your family seems to use violence as a problem-solving tool."

He shifted his large frame, angling so that he bent one leg until his knee brushed her thigh. "Shane carried Taylor out of here because she was being stubborn. And yes," he admitted with a small concession of a grin, "from time to time, my brothers and I get into it, but none of us would ever, ever hit a woman."

She knew her concern was warranted. For any man other than Chandler. But she'd trusted her own intuition, and knew, without a shadow of a doubt that what he said was true. He'd never strike a woman. "You just looked really angry."

"I *am* really angry," he shot back. "So tell me about this Jonas guy and why you've got a restraining order against him."

Lacing her fingers, she clasped her hands in her lap before speaking. "Jonas Black was a patient for a while. He made a pass. I said no. He tried it again. I said no again and referred him to Gavin. Jonas didn't like being what he called, 'handed off,' so he started coming to my office and interrupting my sessions."

"And you didn't think this was relevant?"

"It was more than a year ago," she explained, exasperated. "And Jonas didn't want to hurt me. He wanted to marry me."

"Where is he now?"

"I have no clue."

Chandler stood, tugging her along with him. "C'mon, I need more coffee."

"Me, too," she agreed readily, moving quickly in order to keep pace with his long, smooth strides. Of course, uttering only two syllables was quite safe. Then he wouldn't know that her attention was fixed on his broad shoulders, narrow waist, rounded backside and muscular legs. No sense in letting him know that she was making a meal of him as she followed him into the kitchen.

He didn't know but Shane certainly did. Not expecting to find anyone else around, she hadn't bothered to disguise the open lust in her gaze. At least not before Chandler's younger brother had caught her ogling.

He gave her a wink and a grin that sent color rushing to her cheeks. Lowering her head, she slipped into the closest chair and prayed her adolescent blush would fade before Chandler caught on and called her on it.

"Morning," Shane greeted, locking his hands behind his neck and balancing his seat on the two back legs.

"Good morning." *Please don't let him say anything humiliating.*

"No flirting, Shane," Chandler warned as he re-filled his mug and grabbed a new one off the shelf for Molly.

She was watching everything from the limited field of view allowed by her bowed head. The situation was really, really uncomfortable since she was fairly sure Shane knew Chandler had roused her from sleep by yelling and since the house was sturdy but not soundproofed, he probably heard much of their argument. Was it an argument? she wondered.

Were a few harsh words followed by a pretty reasonable conversation an argument? Had to be. It was the only possible explanation for why she felt so tense. Her spine was stiff, her muscles contracted. Yep, she was a tightly wound pile of nerves right now. So…yep, coffee would help that. Not actually, but she needed something to focus on.

The younger of the two men grinned, bringing a devilish glint to his strikingly clear, blue eyes. Molly relaxed when she no longer felt raging heat on her face and decided it would be okay to lift her head and fully participate in the morning ritual.

Chandler surprised her when he moved to the fridge, splashed some cream in her cup, then placed it in front of her. How did he know how she took her coffee? When had he learned that? "Th-thanks."

"So," Shane began, his tone soft and just on the right side of acceptably flirtatious, "I saw the news

last night. John's a weasel dog who should be shot
and stood up and shot again."

Molly cast a long look at Chandler, then said, "I
don't know where I got the erroneous notion that
any of your brothers had a penchant for violence."

"We've tried to school him," Chandler explained,
"but the poor boy isn't real quick on the uptake, if
you get my drift." Chandler's attempt to muss
Shane's perfectly sleek hair was swatted away. They
slapped hands for a second, then chuckled at their
own silliness.

"I'm smarter than he is," Shane claimed. "Chandler was always the pretty one. The prissy one who
had to have everything just so."

Prissy wasn't a word she might have used, nor,
apparently, was it one Chandler approved either.
He picked up a partially eaten piece of toast and
tossed it at Shane. "I'm not prissy. Sam is prissy."

Shane seemed to accept that. Molly couldn't help
but notice that the brothers seemed to share a bond
she didn't quite understand. She'd had the opportunity to see Chandler and Seth together. It was like
watching two ends of the same rope come together.
Now, here with Shane, she got the same impression.
There was a closeness, almost an anticipation in
their interaction. And above all, it was crystal clear
that these men enjoyed being together.

Molly was perplexed. While she'd never even
considered the plusses of having six siblings, see-

ing Chandler and Shane—hearing them teasingly rag on the absent brothers like great conspirators— made her wonder again what it might be like to have a sister or a brother.

Then again, she knew from her work that siblings could be one another's best friends or fiercest enemies. With her luck, she'd have gotten the latter. Just listening to them, she learned that Clayton and his wife, Tory, were also expecting a child. They lived up in Helena but came down whenever their work schedules permitted. Likewise, brother Cody was there in spirit if not in body, and he called every chance he got. He was some sort of Federal agent currently guarding a witness someplace that no one knew about. Seth and Sam were all at the hospital with their wives, waiting for the arrival of Chance and Val's baby.

"If she delivers at ten, the pot is mine," Shane announced, gleefully rubbing his hands together.

"Pot?" she asked.

"We make friendly wagers," Chandler explained.

"I hope you're still feeling friendly when you have to cough up a hundred bucks. I've got to check on some stock. My cell's on, keep me posted."

Shane left through a back door that was just off plumb enough to stick at the bottom left corner. She heard him curse, then mumble something about needed to fix that, before he stepped out.

The door closed, but not before allowing a rush of clean, cool air into the room.

"I can't believe you all wager on when your nieces and nephews will be born."

"Not when," Chandler explained as if he was teaching the basics of cold fusion. "That's a sucker bet. The whole sex, date, time and weight of the baby thing leaves too much to chance. So, we developed a more sophisticated system."

She found herself loosening up as she listened to the soothing cadence of his voice. "Still seems kind of…I don't know…"

"Childish?" he suggested, mirth dancing in the dark depths of his eyes.

"That, and it puts a lot of pressure on Val, I'm guessing. I wouldn't want to be in the throes of childbirth knowing the adult males in my life were slapping down bets with each scream. There's also something untoward about profiting from the pain of bringing forth new life."

He chuckled and wrapped his large hands around the circumference of his mug. "We don't profit. It's more about the bragging rights."

She lifted her chin, challenging him. "A hundred dollars buys a lot of bragging rights, does it?"

"The winner buys the first savings bond with his proceeds."

Nice touch. So nice in fact that Molly heard the answer with her heart more than her ears. That wasn't so good, was it? It seemed like the more she got to know Chandler Landry, the more she liked and respected him. Very dangerous territory. Not to mention piss-poor timing. She could have laughed at the absurd irony of it. She was genuinely attracted to him. Impressed as all get-out. Completely willing to retract her initial impression of him now. And yet there was the very scary threat of unpredictable John hanging over their heads.

So, the best possible course of action was to find out who John was, get him arrested and then she'd be free to…what? And therein lay the problem. On the one hand she could argue that Chandler was a complex man—and sexier than sin—who was the closest thing to her Prince Charming. He embodied almost all the qualities she would request if she was building the perfect mate from scratch.

But he wasn't a fantasy. He was a real man with a life that couldn't be more different from the path she had so carefully constructed for herself. The money didn't really seem like such a big deal now. The Landrys didn't seem to flaunt their wealth, and the family members she'd spent time with were unpretentious and down to earth. But there were so many of them.

Between brothers, wives and children, the Landrys were on the verge of multiplying to the point of needing their own zip code. And everyone seemed to know everybody else's business. That was the rub. Maybe, *maybe,* she could see herself sharing the most intimate details of her life with a small group of in-laws. But life with Chandler didn't include that option. Marry one and you married them all.

Hello? Her brain called. You're weighing him as marriage material when he hasn't indicated any interest beyond toe-curling but noncommittal sex? And she was a few steps away from selecting a fictional china pattern for her fantasy relationship. This was getting too complicated, too confusing, and it was all happening too fast.

"I'm not used to people zoning out when I talk," he teased as he tapped the table in front of her.

Molly emerged from her thoughts feeling confused and oddly sad. Chandler might have more items in the perfect column of her chart of needs, but none of that could trump the hard fact that he was a temporary guy in her forever fantasy.

"Sorry, I was just trying to work a few things out in my mind."

"And?"

"Still pondering," she told him, believing evasive was the way to go. At least for now.

Their cell phones rang in concert. Chandler answered his, but Molly was forced to call, "Hang on," into her static-clogged line as she ran for the back door.

She not only had to go outside, but she was forced to walk around to the side of the house before her cost-saving service cleared. "Hello?"

"Dr. Jameson, I know I'm only supposed to use this number for emergencies, but believe me, this qualifies."

Recognizing the voice of Bob LaBrett, she pressed her finger against her free ear in order to hear better. "Yes, Mr. LaBrett? What can I do for you?"

"I didn't get the message about my appointment being canceled until after I got here."

"You're at my office?"

"I am, and…well…I think you should get over here immediately."

"What's wrong?"

"I can't describe it. You really have to come."

"Call the sheriff's office," she instructed as fear crept into her mind. Was someone else dead? Hurt? *Oh, God!* "Hang up and call now."

"I know I should have done that first, but I panicked."

"Take a deep breath, Mr. LaBrett." Molly heeded her own advice. "Tell me what the problem is."

"I went to the office for my appointment and there was a package on the doorstep. I picked it up thinking it was a regular delivery. But it isn't."

"What is it?"

"A bomb."

Chapter Twelve

"The man will probably faint if someone doesn't help him soon," Molly told Chandler for the third time since they'd raced from the ranch.

"Seth called the state guys. The bomb squad will probably be there before us." Chandler only hoped that was the truth. "How loony is this guy LaBrett?"

"He isn't loony," she replied, definite censure in her tone. "He happens to be a sweet guy who suffers from debilitating panic attacks. It's taken me three years to get him to a point where we could meet at my office."

"Before that?" Chandler asked as he broke any number of traffic laws speeding toward town.

"I had to do home visits. He was paralyzed by the attacks and too fearful to leave his house."

"Great," Chandler snorted, raking his hands through his hair. "Just the kind of guy you want holding a bomb that's rigged to go off if bent, spindled or mutilated."

The next hour went by in a blur of confusion and

frenetic activity. Chandler was sidelined for most of it, a designation that rankled to no end.

And now he was watching, uselessly, as Molly was tugging on a large, padded bomb suit. "I want to go with her."

"Too dangerous," Seth cautioned. "I'm not thrilled about it either, but LaBrett has already wet his pants. She's our best hope right now for calming the guy down."

She resembled a brown dough boy and walked a lot like a robot from a low-budget horror movie. Not walked, actually, it was more as though she was teetering from side to side. Her arms dangled straight out from her body at a strange angle. Forward motion was slow, hindered by the suit and the trio of men walking with her. At least, he thought they were men. The shielded head gear and bulky suits made it almost impossible to decipher gender.

His foot tapped nervously and relentlessly as he shoved his sunglasses higher on the bridge of his nose. His heart was racing. He could feel tiny droplets of sweat between his shoulderblades, and his throat had gone completely dry.

Sucking in a long breath, he realized the air was perfumed by the flowers planted along the entrance to her office complex. It seemed wrong for such a pleasant scent to be present in the midst of such a dangerous situation. But then, this was all wrong. He was watch-

ing events unfold from more than fifty yards away.
Watching Molly put herself in harm's way.

"I should have gone with her."

"I know this is tough," Seth remarked as he lifted
binoculars to his eyes, "but Molly made sense. If
lots of people freak the guy out, then the fewer people in direct contact with the poor guy, the better."

"Easy for you to say," Chandler countered, feeling
every muscle in his body coil as she got within twenty
feet of the nearly hysterical man. "You're not her—
Not her—" *What? What was he?* "You're just *not.*"

"That was eloquently put, maybe you should
think about a career in television."

"You don't want to bait me right now," Chandler
warned.

"I'd rather have you mad at me than chasing
after her."

While he was sure somewhere down the line he'd
appreciate that touching moment of brotherly love,
now wasn't that moment. Not when Molly had
reached the man holding the bomb.

Molly could hardly breathe. The suit was tight
and so padded that it made even simple movements
a challenge. The face shield wasn't helping, either.
It was thick, distorting her vision, but most disturbing, it was scratched. She didn't want to know that
things did explode, marking the protective gear
that—she shivered at the memory—according to
the team leader was "her best protective option."

Not *complete* protection; not *totally* protective; just her best option. She gulped in air. Did that mean that in the event the device went off she'd only be maimed and not killed? What *exactly* did "best protective option" mean?

Get it together, the little voice in her head demanded.

"Mr. LaBrett?" she began in the most soothing tone she could muster. "Bob? Look at me."

The man was drenched in sweat, clutching a box the size of a couple of loaves of bread, crudely wrapped in brown paper and tied with twine.

His wide, terrified eyes met hers. His shoulders shook as he continued to sob. Seeing his tear-stained cheeks and red, runny nose nearly broke her heart. "Bob? These men are going to help you, but you have to listen very carefully to their instructions. Can you do that?"

"Uh-huh," he said after a few sniffles.

Bomb squad member one stepped forward, using some sort of fancy hand-held thing to X-ray the box. The other two were busy wrapping Bob in some sort of blanket and placing one of the shield things on his head.

"It's going to be okay," Molly said.

"No it won't," Bob argued, his voice cracking. "I don't want to die."

"None of us do," Molly promised him. "It won't be that much longer. You're doing great."

"I wet myself," Bob sobbed. "Twice."

"None of us care. We all know how stressful this has been for you. You're doing great. These guys will figure out the best possible solution and until they do, I'll be right here with you."

"It…had…your…picture…on…it," Bob whimpered.

Her eyes flickered down to the box. Sure enough, her picture was in the lower right-hand corner. Chandler's was opposite. Her heart skipped when she realized when the photos were taken. Last night. Outside the warehouse/studio.

Can't think about that now. "Have you been doing your assignments?" she asked.

"I, um, went to a park last week. I know I was supposed to stay for ten minutes. I stayed for five." His speech was fast, probably mirroring his heart rate. A very typical symptom of a major panic episode.

"Good. That's a start."

"If I don't die, I'll go back for the whole ten minutes."

"I'm going to hold you to that," Molly promised. "Deep breathing, Bob. In and out."

"My throat feels like it's closing."

"But it won't," Molly assured him. "Just focus on me and control your breathing. In and out."

They spent the next tense half hour like that. Molly giving hypnotic, repetitive directions to quivering Bob while the bomb squad worked diligently to find a way to separate her patient from the bomb.

Finally she was told, "We're going to make the transfer." The squad member was pulling what looked like heavy-duty pot holders onto his hands. "I'll need you to go back behind the tape line now."

She read the fear in Bob's eyes, then shook her head. "I'm staying with my patient."

"Can't let you do that, Doctor. We have protocols."

She shifted her gaze from Bob's somewhat calmer face to the officer. "I don't give a fig if you have a declaration from the governor. You do your job and let me do mine."

He turned and sternly warned, "This isn't like handing off a football, lady." He lowered his voice, probably to keep Bob from going into another crying jag. "I can't guarantee the thing won't blow."

"I don't remember asking you for assurances. Let's get on with it, shall we?"

"This is a violation of procedure," he grumbled.

"Get over it." She waddled to the left a little, making sure Bob could see her face, hoping he didn't read the fear she was struggling to keep at bay. It was a tense and difficult few minutes as the bomb squad walked them through what would happen.

"Did you hear that?" Molly asked. "You wait until he tells you to let go."

"Got it," Bob replied, somewhat calmer.

Each move was calculated and carefully executed. One squad member was down on his knees, holding some sort of container just below the package. Another guy held the X-ray thing and seemed to be giving the directions. The one wearing the industrial pot holders was actually effecting the transfer.

Molly smelled her own fear and fought the very real urge to turn and run. "A few more minutes," she told Bob. "They're almost finished. Deep breaths."

"Okay, pal," the officer began, slipping his protected hands just below Bob's. "I'm going to count to three, and then you *slowly* release the package. Remember, *slowly.*"

"I…I don't think I can," Bob whimpered. "I'm scared."

"We all are," Molly assured him. "You can do this, Bob."

"I can't."

"Yes, you can. He's going to count now, Bob. Listen to his voice."

"O-okay."

"One."

Molly's breath caught in her throat.

"Two"

A trickle of sweat dripped down from her temple.

"Three."

She closed her eyes, steeled for disaster.

Nothing.

Her eyes flew open, and she discovered that the package had been extracted and was now in the possession of the trained professional. She breathed a huge sigh as the team of three took the package and began the long walk back toward the specially designed vehicle.

Bob leaned back against the building, then slowly slid down in a heap.

"You did it," Molly said as she knelt next to him, patting his shoulder. "You're a hero, Bob."

"I…I just want to go home."

After removing her head gear and his, she impulsively leaned closer and kissed his flushed cheek. "Thank you."

"I think I'm going to be sick."

"WHAT WERE YOU THINKING?" Chandler demanded as soon as he'd sprinted from the safe area to where she was stripping off the hot protective suit.

He stood crowding her, watching as she slipped her fingers through her hair, shaking the wheat-colored strands into a loose, wild mass.

Her shirt clung to her, damp with perspiration. It appeared her slacks hadn't fared much better. They were crumpled from the bomb suit. But what he noticed most of all was the tremor in her hands.

He felt like a jerk for yelling at her. But he'd

been so worried and so damned helpless standing behind the caution barrier with nothing to do but watch…and worry, damn it.

Not caring about rules or deals, he wrapped his arms around her and pulled her against him. Placing several kisses on top of her head, he simply rubbed her back until he no longer felt her small body trembling. While she had ignited his temper by putting herself so close to danger, he had to admire her moxie. He bet there weren't too many women who would go toe-to-toe with a live bomb, regardless of the circumstances.

"I'm disgusting," she mumbled against his shirt. "I need a shower."

"Easily done," he promised. "Hey, Seth!"

His brother came over and asked, "How are you doing, Molly?"

"I feel like I spent an hour in a sauna wearing a parka."

She pulled out of his embrace, leaving Chandler feeling oddly empty. "I'm going to take her back to the ranch. You need anything before we go?"

"I'll be by later." Seth tipped his hat to Molly, then offered Chandler a brotherly nod. He turned back to the huddle of law enforcement types, then stopped and spun around. "By the way, Chance and Val had a girl. Chloe Elizabeth Landry weighed in at seven pounds, five ounces when she arrived at twelve-o-five."

In unison they said, "Cody won."

"Congratulations," Molly offered as they slowly made their way to the SUV.

Several reporters rushed them as they crossed under the yellow crime-scene tape. Chandler immediately shielded her, using his bulk to muscle them through the small throng.

"These will be some lovely photographs," Molly joked once they were safely inside the car. Tinted windows thwarted any further attempts at capturing the moment on film. "I've always dreamed of having my picture in the paper when I look like something the cat dragged in and spit out."

"You don't look that bad," he offered, touching the soft underside of her chin to tilt her face to him. "In fact, I think you're beautiful."

She gave a nervous little laugh. "Then you've spent too much time in the gym. I need a long soak, then I should probably come back and check on Bob LaBrett."

"Seth had him driven home."

"Good," she sighed, turning away from him to look out the front windshield.

He started the engine, then navigated carefully through the maze of onlookers. His cell phone rang again. And just as he had for the past hour, he checked the identifying information and didn't answer.

"That could be important," Molly prodded.

"It's Mike," he said.

"You're blowing off your boss?"

"He's pissed at me."

"For what?"

He liked the little twinge of indignation in her voice. It might mean that she had some feelings for him. *But what feelings and why did it matter?* He wasn't sure, he just knew that it did. The memory of her approaching that bomb made that perfectly clear to him. It mattered. She mattered.

"I, uh, kind of refused to cover the story."

"Cover the story? He expected you to roll film, maybe get footage of people being blown to hell and back?"

"It's what we do," he explained, wondering why the explanation rang hollow in his own ears. "Well, it might be what I *used* to do."

She made a small sound. A small, shocked intake of air. "He might fire you?"

"Actually, he did."

He nearly jumped when her hand reached out and closed on his forearm. It was one of the rare times when she instituted physical contact.

"He can't do that! You're…you're famous."

He allowed a chuckle to rumble around in his throat. "Hardly. Mike might come around, but if he doesn't, that's okay too. I've got a few other irons in the fire."

"But it's wrong," she huffed, squeezing his arm to punctuate the remark.

"Not really," Chandler admitted. "I'm supposed to report the story, Molly. Not *be* it."

"You didn't choose this." She withdrew her hand. "I can't believe this has cost you your job. I'm sorry."

He shrugged. "I lost a job. Mrs. Zarnowski and John's mother are dead. Deputy McClain is hurt. Your house is nothing but rubble and ash and my car is twisted metal. All in all, I'd say I'm still way ahead of the game."

He grinned when he heard her rather colorful comparison between John and a male body part. "Did you see the wrapping?"

"No. Why?"

"The bomb had our pictures on it. From last night."

His heart skipped. "When last night?"

"The warehouse," she explained. "They were grainy, so I'm thinking they were taken with one of those zoom lenses, but nonetheless, John was there."

"Dammit. The place was crawling with cops and he still managed to get pictures?"

"I know. But that tells us two things."

"It does?"

"Sure," her voice was strong, confident. "John has to be local or have a decent knowledge of the area. That's the only way he would have known about the warehouse."

"Right. Good. What's the other thing?"

"He's fearless."

"That doesn't sound good."

"It isn't."

Chapter Thirteen

A freshly bathed Molly slipped a casual dress over her head. The sleeveless garment fell just above her knees, and the green color, she decided as she glanced at her reflection, complemented her eyes. She grabbed a sweater from the closet, slipped on her new, strappy sandals and decided that she'd have to shop again soon. She was going through outfits faster than a messy toddler.

Hurrying with her watch and the simple gold earrings that now represented her entire line of accessories, she bounded toward the stairs. Chandler was in a rush to meet his new niece.

Her stomach growled but she ignored it, silently promising herself a special treat from the first vending machine they encountered.

She hadn't touched or held a newborn since her pediatrics rotation, so she felt excited and giddy at the prospect. Of course, she knew that it was an overreaction to her current situation. The past few days had been about death and violence. Going to see a new baby was the absolute antithesis of those experiences.

Chandler had changed clothing, as well. He looked so different that she actually stopped just shy of the bottom step and didn't bother to even try to keep her mouth from gaping open. It was the first time she'd ever seen him in jeans. Well, jeans didn't quite capture it. Nope, it was much more like a second skin of soft, faded denim. A shoulder-hugging, pale-ecru shirt was tucked neatly into the belted waistband of his pants. Completing the outfit was a pair of Italian leather loafers that she'd bet cost about a month's pay. All in all, he had a kind of high-end cowboy thing going on, and it was quite an impressive package.

"Have I grown a third arm?" he teased, those chocolate eyes sparkling amusement.

"I just didn't expect you to be a dress-down kind of guy."

His dark head tilted to the side as he regarded her for several long, electrifying seconds. "Speaking of dress, yours is lovely."

She gave an exaggerated curtsy. "Thank you. If I'm overdone, I can change into something else."

"Definitely not," he insisted, offering his hand. "But I'm afraid no one will notice the baby with you in the room."

She smiled, taking his hand and marveling at the

feel of his warm skin. The tight coil of desire in her stomach responded, as well. Though she was getting more used to the feeling. All it took for her to get hot and bothered at this point was a whiff of his subtle cologne. The man smelled wonderful.

Though the day had gotten off to a horrible start, the afternoon blended into early evening with Molly's spirits riding high. Her whole world had been upended, yet she couldn't recall ever being as happy as she was, going hand in hand with him out to the car. There was a contentment being with him, a *rightness* she hadn't felt before. And all of this was happening in the middle of the most bizarre and frightening chapter in her life. How was that possible?

"Seth called while you were primping."

She feigned indignation. "I do not primp. I'm far too practical to primp."

"You're practical? Have you forgotten that I saw you power shop yesterday?"

"That was an exception," she insisted, grinning like some teenager on her first real date. "I didn't think it was a good idea to linger in public."

"It isn't," Chandler agreed. "Seth has stationed two deputies at the hospital. One will be our escort, the other will guard the car just in case John is lurking about."

Molly's magical, girlish moment was over. Hearing John's name was enough to douse her mood instantly. "I was thinking while I was—"

"Primping."

She cast him a sidelong glance. "*Bathing.* I've been racking my brain trying to think of some reason why someone would go to this much trouble to punish me. It really doesn't make any sense."

"Seth is trying to track down Jonas Black. So far, no luck. The guy doesn't seem to have a steady work history."

"He wouldn't," Molly agreed, twisting several strands of her hair between her thumb and forefinger as her mind mulled the possibilities. "Jonas was a very troubled guy. His mother was on her fourth husband by the time he started school. He'd been abused by a couple of stepfathers and pseudo-stepfathers before finally dropping out of high school. I have to tell you, I don't see Jonas doing any of this."

"Why? He stalked you."

"Not to be unkind, but he wasn't that bright. Whoever is doing this is no slouch in the smarts department."

"Maybe he's been studying up in the year and a half since you last saw him."

She shook her head. "There's the time factor, as well. Why wait all this time? We both know that a woman is most in danger at the time a relationship ends and/or when a restraining order is issued. Once Jonas was served with the order, he simply disappeared. If he was truly fixated and not disturbed, he would have reacted then, not now."

"You're probably right, but until Seth tracks him down, I'm not willing to give him a pass."

"I know Jonas's voice," she continued. "John and Jonas are not the same person. Jonas is in his late thirties. John is too young."

"I know you don't want to hear this, but I'm sure this is somehow connected to your work. You have a virtual parade of unbalanced people marching through your office."

She bristled slightly. A week ago she would have launched into a stern lecture on how misunderstood the mentally ill were and how cruel and unfair it was to lump them all into the very minute minority of truly dangerous individuals. That was two dead bodies and three bombs ago.

Speaking of which. "Was there anything about the latest bomb that the police found useful?"

"Yeah, it was studded."

"Studded?" She wasn't sure what that was but it didn't sound good.

"C-4 again, only this time John spiked the explosive with shrapnel and nails to maximize the effect."

Rubbing her upper arms, she staved off a fearful shiver. "Escalating violence usually means the bomber is feeling invincible. He's growing bolder because he's gotten away with so much already."

"Nothing like excelling at your work to make a guy feel over confident."

"Don't laugh, but in a book I read, the hero used the villain's brazen behavior to his advantage. Wyatt drew the guy out by publically criticizing him. The villain was so mad at having his criminal skills questioned, he decided to stage a more impressive crime. Wyatt planned for that and was able to catch the bad guy before he could hurt anyone else." Including the lovely scientist who'd invented a way to change weather patterns. Okay, so it sounded fanciful when she said it out loud, but the book was really good. She'd finished it in one sitting.

"That's fiction," Chandler dismissed. "This is reality, so don't go thinking you're going to play Wonder Woman."

"Then help me think of something before John decides to strike again," she said angrily. "So far all I know is that he's a young guy who killed his mother. He's got a thing for the number thirteen and he's handy with explosives. He lives alone or has access to a completely private location. Work?" She paused to ponder that aspect. "He's too mobile to have a steady job. He's got the time and patience to study and follow both of us and has more than a working knowledge of Jasper."

"You're forgetting something."

"What?"

"He may have a thing for the number thirteen but he's got a *serious* jones for you."

"For both of us," she argued. "Okay, so maybe

most of his anger is directed at me, but he wouldn't have blown up your car without a reason. Twisted, I'll grant you, but he was definitely sending you a message."

"He hated my car?"

She smiled in spite of herself. It was nice that he had the ability to make her laugh even in the face of a terrible situation.

"Maybe he hates anyone you're connected to," she said in a rush, taking a mental walk in a new direction. "What if we're looking at this all wrong? John called *your* show. I wasn't a target of anything until I did the call-in, and I was a last-minute replacement. John is now taunting *your* guest. John put *your* picture on the last bomb alongside mine. Maybe…what if John is avenging some wrong he perceives you committed?"

"That doesn't make a lot of sense," he cautioned. "That plan has small hope of success because too much is left to chance. John'd have no way of knowing that messing with you would make me crazy."

"He would if he knew a lot about you," she pressed. "Think about it. If John had studied you, or even got inside information about you, it would explain how he found the secret warehouse. Have you used that location before?"

He nodded. "A couple of times. I interviewed one of the victims of the Lakeside rapist there. Do you remember the case?"

"Of course," Molly answered. "There wasn't a woman within two hundred miles of the lake that wasn't scared snotless."

"Snotless?" he repeated with a snicker.

"The guy kidnapped, raped and tortured, bound and blindfolded women for days on end. He was caught because his last victim was able to give a general location where she'd been held captive, and smart enough to make sure she left her fingerprints on the underside of the toilet seat."

"She was an amazing young woman," Chandler agreed. "She was only seventeen but she managed to give the police enough leads to track down, arrest and convict that disgusting bastard."

She heard the venom in his voice and had to agree with his assessment. "Wasn't the rapist some sort of real estate broker?"

"Yep. He used the vacant homes of his unsuspecting clients. That was one of the reasons the cops had such a hard time. He kept moving the crime scenes. Of course, that backfired big-time because the last victim's mother was an interior decorator. It turned out the mother had taken photographs of the very home the rapist held her daughter."

"What are the odds?" Molly wondered, feeling a rush of empathy for the poor girl. Hopefully she was getting appropriate therapy to help her deal with such a trauma.

"Slim to none," Chandler agreed. "Anyway, the

girl recognized the carpeting and crown molding—the only things she'd seen because of the blindfold."

"How could someone so young show so much inner strength?" she mused.

"She's a strong girl with a supportive mother who I'm sure will do everything in her power to help her heal."

Molly hoped so. "Was that the only time you've been to that location?"

"No. I taped another interview there about five years ago. The foreman of the Steadman Ranch. He'd been video and audio taping the abuses of publicly held lands for months and was about to testify before the Bureau of Land Management and Congress. He didn't want the Steadmans to know he was the mole until the Feds organized his relocation."

Molly was perplexed. She knew the rapist had been given a sentence of several lifetimes, so he couldn't be John. The Steadman thing was a possibility. "Did the guy relocate?"

He nodded, steering the SUV into the back entrance of the hospital where the uniformed deputies stood waiting. "My brother Cody handled the relocation personally. The Steadmans got a hand-slap of fines, but last I heard, they're still in business."

"What about something personal?" Molly queried after they left the car under the watchful eyes of the deputy.

Chandler held the door for her, breathing in the floral scent of her hair as she passed beneath his arm. He liked the way the dress hugged her shape. He noticed two orderlies watching her, too, and it didn't sit well.

Nope. Not at all. In fact, he thought he was exercising incredible restraint when he didn't punch the twenty-something orderly who was practically drooling after his beady little eyes spent a little too much time on her breasts. *Twit.*

"G'morning," the little jerk offered, puffing his chest out as Molly passed him.

Even though he'd dated some pretty stunning women in his life, he'd never experienced such a real and palpable surge of jealousy. Oh, he wanted to tell himself that his concern was pure, borne of his very genuine concern for her safety. But the truth was, he didn't want that man—hell, *any* man—looking at Molly with such open, sweeping lust.

Because he knew exactly how the guy felt. That was the most annoying part. He knew the guy was probably undressing her with his eyes. Wondering, none-too-subtly, whether her skin was as soft and smooth as it looked. Or how his hands could easily encircle her waist. Or how he longed to feel the weight of her breast against his palm.

Molly stopped suddenly and asked, "Are you excited?"

"So much it almost hurts," he answered, unable to make eye contact.

"I'm going to enjoy this," she chattered, following the pink-and-blue stripe painted on the floor to direct visitors to the maternity area. "I can't remember the last time I held an infant." She glanced over her shoulder to ask, "Do you think Val will let me hold the baby? Or is that presumptuous? It probably is. In fact, I should wait outside. This is a family moment and I don't want to—"

Chandler couldn't stand it anymore. Instead of hearing her words, he was fixated on her mouth. He reached out, catching Molly around the midsection and spinning her into him. His fingers tangled in her hair as he insistently positioned her head and brushed his lips to hers.

He'd told himself it would be just a brief exchange. A small sip of water for a thirsty man. It didn't turn out that way.

The minute his mouth found hers, he wanted more. Without breaking the bond, he moved her deeper into the alcove, his hands moving from her shoulders up to cradle her face. His breath caught when her palms flattened against his stomach. He waited, scared she would push him away, afraid of what might happen if she didn't.

His eyes fluttered closed while he tested the seam of her lips with his tongue. Chandler pressed against her, allowing his body to be imprinted with the feel of every curve, every sweet inch of her.

His thumbs made slow, meaningful circles against her cheeks as he deepened the kiss. The cool taste of mint was a sharp contrast to the hot, moistness of her mouth. It wasn't enough. He couldn't seem to get close enough. Especially not when she moved—fractionally—but enough to inspire a new, strong wave of desire to surge through him. Slowly, calculatingly, he let his fingers slide down, exploring the line of her jaw, then lower still, to the pulse point at her throat.

At his tentative exploration, a small moan rumbled in her throat, nearly sending him over the edge. He knew he should stop. But knowing and doing were two completely different things. Chandler knew it would be easier to stop breathing than to pull away from the sweet slice of heaven he'd found with Molly.

And he did stop breathing. From shock. He hadn't expected to feel a hand gripping his shoulder or the urgent and annoying shake.

"This is a public place, kids. Separate or get a room."

Chandler recognized Chance's voice and for an instant wondered if Val would mind raising their baby daughter alone because he'd gladly kill his own brother just then.

Tucking Molly's head against his chest so she

could regain her composure, he turned and found his scowl instantly erased by the beaming, proud light shining in Chance's eyes. "I was in the middle of something," he joked. "Is everything about you?"

Reluctantly Chandler released Molly and gave his brother a hearty, back-slapping hug. "Well done, Chance. Congratulations."

"She's beautiful," he gushed.

Chandler had to smile. He couldn't recall Chance ever gushing. Apparently fatherhood had made him into a girl. "Takes after Val, huh?"

Chance's expression was euphoric. "For the most part, though she has the trademark Landry black hair." He peered around Chandler and added, "Hi, Molly."

"Dr. Landry," she responded in a small voice.

"Chance," he corrected, shoving Chandler away to engulf a stunned Molly in a bear hug. "If you're going to share spit with my brother, we should be on a first-name basis, don't you think?"

"Um…sure," she stammered.

Chance took Molly by the hand, almost dragging her down the hallway. Chandler followed closely behind. The deputy behind him.

The sounds of celebratory Landrys left no question as to which room was Val's. Chandler touched his lips, then raked his fingers through his hair as he braced for the predictable round of hugs, slaps and high-fives.

Molly wasn't as well prepared. In fact, she wasn't prepared at all. Landrys were, she decided, a lot like a pack of dogs. She was suddenly surrounded by large, loud men wearing big, silly grins. Still, the smiles were deceptive. She didn't miss the quiet curiosity directed at her from five pairs of male eyes. And she was sure that the women she couldn't see beyond the Landry huddle were equally inquisitive.

Introductions were made and friendships renewed. Molly found the scene intimidating as all get-out. Of course, it didn't help that her brain had been drained of all cognitive ability by his kiss. Or that her legs were still shaky these several minutes later. The small room was no match for the formidable clan. Every available inch of space around the bed was occupied by some member of the family.

Val looked tired but thrilled. She positively glowed as she peered down at the tiny infant cradled in her arms. Callie and Taylor flanked Val, taking turns folding down the pink blanket in order to get a better look at the baby. Molly remained back from the group, watching and listening to the fragments of conversations.

She nearly missed the woman seated in a chair in the corner. But the room was full beyond capacity, and the woman had been hidden by the rowdy group of men. She hoisted herself out of the chair, awkwardly trying to balance her huge belly against the forces of nature. It seemed impossible that such a tiny woman could be *that* pregnant.

"I'm Tory," she greeted with a big smile. "My husband is that one," she pointed to the only man Molly hadn't previously met. "Clayton learned his manners in prison. I don't have any excuses for the rest of them."

"Nice to meet you," Molly returned. *Prison?* Yes. She remembered that. The man had been wrongly convicted.

"Don't be shy," Val yelled over the din of male voices. "Come meet little Chloe."

Molly felt her eyes grow wide but she remained planted in the spot.

"Make way," Taylor instructed, shoving Chandler and two other brothers aside. "C'mon, Molly, she's really sweet."

It wasn't as if she'd have a choice. Suddenly someone had a grip on her wrist, and she was positioned bedside, with Val lifting the squirming child toward her.

Molly melted. Positively melted. The scrunched little face beneath the tiny pink hat threatened to bring tears to her eyes. With utmost care, she took the baby and held her close. Suddenly she was cooing and whispering and totally engrossed in the perfection of this new life.

"She's precious," Molly said, not taking her eyes off the little fingers gripping her pinkie.

"She is," Val agreed. "I'm liking her a whole lot more now that she's on the outside."

"You'll forget," Chance told his wife.

"Sure I will," Val replied sarcastically. "And you're basing that on giving birth how many times?"

Molly was barely aware of a cell phone ringing. It wasn't until her purse was passed, assembly-line style, from Landry to Landry to her, that she realized it was hers.

"Want me to get it for you?" Taylor asked, fishing the phone out of the bag after Molly nodded.

Taylor flipped it open, then held it up so Molly could speak. "Hello?"

There was static and scratching and the muffled sound of words she couldn't quite make out.

"Could you speak up, please?"

As if prearranged, the room went suddenly quiet. Molly repeated her request. "We've got a lousy connection. Hello? This is Dr. Jameson."

A familiar voice came over the line. "Be sure to kiss the baby for me."

Chapter Fourteen

"I know John's call upset you, but try not to let it get to you," Chandler counseled as they went out and reclaimed the SUV. He passed each deputy a cigar with a pink band before thanking them and settling into the driver's seat.

"I'm not upset, I'm pissed off," she insisted, crossing her arms and glaring out the window.

"Is that a medical term?" he joked.

Molly felt some of her ire slip away. How did he do that? "I was having a perfectly wonderful time holding the baby and he screwed that up."

"I was surprised," Chandler remarked.

Molly regarded him for a second before saying, "I know. I have no idea how he got my cell number. I'll call my friend Claire. She's a computer whiz, maybe she can find out if the number is out in cyberspace because it really—"

"About that, too, I guess," he cut in. "I was talking about you and the baby. I didn't have you pegged as the baby type."

"I'm not. I mean, I like babies. Babies are cute. I've just never given the idea much thought." She didn't like the way his brow furrowed. "What?"

"No thought? Aren't you about the right age to start hearing the tick-tock of your biological clock?"

"I hit the snooze button a few years ago."

He tossed his dark head back and laughed.

"What about you?" she countered. "Isn't there some law requiring X number of offspring from each and every Landry?"

"I hope not," Chandler admitted with an exaggerated flinch for effect. "But in answer to your question, of course I've thought about it."

"And?" *Why am I asking him? How is it any of my business? Who cares, I want to know.*

"It's part of my someday."

"Your 'someday'?"

He shrugged and let out a slow breath. "You know, someday I'll learn to snowboard. Someday I'll figure out how to program the timer on my VCR. Someday I'll write a book. Someday I'll get married and have kids."

"Wait," she said on an excited rush of air. "You want to write?"

Chandler's expression flashed, then closed. "I was just giving a hypothetical list. I know how to snowboard, and I can program my VCR in under a minute."

Molly wasn't buying it. She remembered how she had secretly longed to try her hand at writing. The thought of having her books used as references by millions of people still gave her chills. And she was well on her way. Okay, maybe on her way to thousands, but still, she had a dream and she was fairly sure she sensed he, too, had a creative side not yet tapped.

"Since you're currently unemployed and you don't need an income, why not try your hand at writing?"

"Who said I wanted to write?" he asked, clearly annoyed.

"You did." She tucked her leg beneath her and stared at his handsome profile. He reminded her of a film-noir hero, dark and mysterious in the uneven shadows cast by the streetlamps as they headed back toward the ranch.

"I didn't. Can we drop it?"

"In a minute," she continued. "I could help you. I have a decent agent in New Orleans. She does fiction as well as nonfiction. I'm sure if I called her, she'd be willing to look at an outline or synopsis or whatever. She could also give you some tips about markets, opportunities—"

"Give it a rest, Molly."

She smiled in the dark. He had the bug; she could tell. She'd listened to enough people in the throes of denial to recognize it in him. Given that he'd opened his home to her, the least she could do was nudge him in the direction he secretly wanted to go. That's what friends did for each other.

Not friends, that nagging voice in her head corrected. That's what *wives* did.

She could not—correction—*would* not go down that road. A rational, reasonable person did not contemplate marriage to a man she'd known for less than a week. And *known* was a stretch. In fact, she thought as she settled against the seat, he was a virtual stranger. That realization was frustrating. As was the certain knowledge that she wanted to know him. Good or bad, the John situation would play out and there would be nothing left keeping her and Chandler together.

That left her with an important decision to make. Enjoy it while she could or stay safe. Safe was the smarter option, but her heart pleaded with her to take a risk. Just this one time. Scared and excited all at once, she took a breath and asked, "Do you still want to know why I became a shrink?"

He glanced over at her for a second, taken aback by her sudden offering to share something—anything—about herself. Chandler had almost gotten used to prying evasive answers from her. "Uh, sure. Yes."

"As hokey as it sounds, I wanted to help people."

"That's not hokey," he assured her. "Chance felt the same way. I completely understand that need."

"There's a reason why I have the need, though."

He heard her take a fortifying lungful of oxygen and figured whatever she was about to tell him was major. He just didn't know if it was serious major or something major only to her. Several seconds passed and she didn't speak. Gently he prodded her. "Am I supposed to guess?"

Hearing her small laugh put him at ease. He liked that he could read her mood. Liked that she seemed to respond to him when she was scared or annoyed.

"My mother," Molly said softly.

He felt the stab at his heart The word brought immediate images of his absent parents to the fore. "You can tell me anything," he told her. But again a long silence followed. "Okay, how about I go first."

"This is hard," Molly admitted. "I'm the one that listens but I don't think I ever realized how hard it is to spill your guts to someone for the first time."

"I'll make it easier. My mother ran off to find herself. My father ran off to find my mother. I guess they found each other and decided they didn't want to be saddled with seven grown sons, a ranch and a small family fortune to control."

"That's horrible," Molly cried, genuine compassion behind the outburst.

Chandler readily agreed. "It was rough for a lot of years. Worse for Shane."

"Because he was the baby?"

"Was?" Chandler joked. "*He* still *is* a baby. Haven't you noticed?"

"He's nice."

He slid his hand over and wrapped his fingers around her knee. If he'd have thought about it, he would have remembered that she wasn't wearing slacks; she was wearing a dress. Which meant his palm was resting atop silken, warm flesh. *Her* flesh. The flesh that led to the *other* flesh. Like the flesh a few inches higher than his hand. His body reacted predictably and uncomfortably and suddenly he knew that the ride to the ranch would feel like a million miles.

"Shane is a great guy," Chandler admitted, glad that he was able to choke out the words in a seemingly normal tone. "All my brothers are great. But, back to the topic at hand. Shane and my father had words, and Shane, being eighteen, cocky and impulsive, ran off. He roamed around for a while before finally coming home. He was ready to make peace with the old man, but that didn't happen. It haunts him."

"Has he gotten some counseling?" Molly inquired gently. "I'd offer myself but I don't think it would be appropriate under the circumstances. Gavin is a wonderful therapist. He often works with people who've—"

"Shane on a shrink's couch? I'd buy tickets to that." His mind flashed a quick image of his youngest brother lying on a couch, lights dimmed, big boots sticking up, and Chandler had to chuckle.

"It isn't a sign of weakness, you know."

Hearing the hurt in her tone, he felt instantly contrite. "You have to know Shane. He yells and blusters but deep down, he's completely harmless. He just wears his heart on his sleeve. I laughed because I couldn't imagine Shane sitting still to let a trained professional examine his psyche. Hell, I don't think Shane even knows he has a psyche."

"Still, I'd be happy to refer him."

"And I'd be happy to stand and watch while you tell him that. Just take my advice, duck if you do."

"Your family is very…strange."

He considered that for a minute, then responded by saying, "Not really. All things considered, I think we're a pretty normal group."

"But there's no privacy."

The ferocity of her remark caught him off guard. "Privacy?"

"Your lives are so…so…intermingled."

He thought for a minute, then agreed wholeheartedly. "We're family. *Real* family. You want to know what dampened my good time back at the hospital?"

"John's call?"

"No," Chandler flexed his fingers against the molded plastic steering wheel. "Cody couldn't be here. I looked around the room and I wanted to see his face."

"I'm sure he had a valid reason for—"

"I'm not mad at him, Molly. He's working and I totally get that he can't leave a witness unprotected. It bummed me out that he missed welcoming little Chloe with the rest of us. Once they're gone, you can't get those times back and, well, when we're all together, we're…complete."

"But don't you…never mind."

"Ask me," he insisted.

"Don't you ever feel closed in by all those people?"

"Sure. Sometimes—rare times, it absolutely sucks. Most of the time it's great to have so many people at your back."

"I suppose it could have its benefits."

He rubbed her knee briefly, then pulled the hem of her dress down and rested his hand on top. "Other than when I was in the service, I've never known what it's like to be lonely. Not in my entire life. Few people can say that."

"I'm an expert on it," Molly admitted. "My parents loved me, but my childhood was really, really, *really* different from yours."

"There were lots of times when I wished I'd been an only child, but truth be told, I wouldn't trade with you for anything."

He felt her muscle tense beneath his touch before she said, "My mother was ill."

"Cancer?" he guessed. An educated guess: she would have been a young woman when she died and cancer explained that.

"Severe, debilitating manic-depression."

He whistled, searching his brain for what little he knew about the disease. "That's tough."

"My dad dealt with it by working eighty hours a week. It was easier for him to remove himself from the situation than to confront it."

"I'm sure he tried."

"He did," she agreed quickly. "He didn't know how to deal with Mom. Or me. He figured if he earned a decent living, kept money in the bank and a roof over our heads, his job was done."

"What was your job?" Chandler inquired gently.

"From as far back as I can remember, I was on suicide watch."

"Wow. Wow," he repeated, not sure what the correct response should be. "That's a tough thing to put a kid through."

"It sounds tough now," she said, reaching down and covering his hand with her smaller one. "Truthfully, though, at the time I didn't know any different. It's hard to miss what you've never had and don't know."

"I can't imagine a small child with that kind of responsibility. That kind of pressure. How'd you handle it?"

"Badly." Her grip tightened. "My mother didn't

just die when I was thirteen, Chandler. She killed herself."

He immediately twisted his wrist, capturing her hand and bringing it to his lips. "I'm sorry, honey. Really. That's a horrible thing for a young girl to suffer through." He tucked her hand against his chest and held it there. If there was comfort or wisdom to be offered, it eluded him at that moment.

"It was partially my fault."

"I don't believe that," Chandler said with complete conviction. "You said she was ill for a long time."

"I was supposed to go straight home from school. My dad would slip medication in her coffee every morning. I know *now* that he was sedating her, but at the time, I thought everyone's mother slept until well into the afternoon."

"You were what? In junior high? Whatever the outcome, your mother made the decision to end her life. No matter how misguided."

She made a small sound—a kind of accepting sigh. Then she explained, "That is very true and I accept that. Guilt-free. Promise. I do, however, have some responsibility because I didn't go straight home that day."

He kissed her knuckles several times. "You were a kid, Molly, Cut yourself some slack."

"I did it for the dumbest of all reasons. I had a crush on this boy. By way of a note passed to friend, who asked another friend to ask my friend if I would meet him at a park near our house, I went straight there about a millisecond after the bell rang."

"You were entitled to a little R & R," Chandler said, feeling her grip get just a tiny bit tighter as she continued to tell her story.

"That's how I justified it. Only, it didn't turn out as expected."

"The guy was a jerk?"

She gave a little self-deprecating laugh. "Worse, he was a no-show."

"Little…weenie."

"You said weenie? After you mocked my use of snotless?"

"I'm being a gentleman," he announced, pressing her hand to his lips and holding it there.

"He didn't show up because the note wasn't from him. He knew nothing about the clandestine meeting. Hell, he didn't even know I existed. It was a prank by the popular girls. You must know them," she teased, tugging at her hand.

Chandler didn't release his hold. For some reason it just felt right to hold some part of her as she shared a pretty intimate part of her life with him. "Knew them, dated them, got dumped by them."

"We all have our crosses to bear. So, Mom dies, and Dad and I are left to build something of a normal life."

"Must have been hard."

"That's the strange part," she admitted, her voice softer now. "It was easier. And I think that ate away at both of us. We never talked, of course. But the honest truth was, he didn't have to avoid coming home anymore. I could have friends over and not worry that my crazy mother would come out an humiliate me. It was pretty…normal."

"Good."

"For me, yes. My dad started drinking eventually. I've always wondered how he managed to stay sober all those years when my mother's behavior was completely unpredictable, and it was only years after she died that he crawled inside a bottle."

"You know," he began, pressing her hand over his heart, "I'm feeling like five kinds of a fool for griping about my folks. Compared to what you went through, my life has been a cake walk."

"I'm not some tortured soul, Chandler. I made peace with what happened long ago. When my dad died, my only regret was that we'd never been able to establish any kind of relationship as adults. I didn't care about his failings as a parent, but I would like to have *known* him. You know?"

"Yep. I was lucky in that respect. My folks got a glimpse of the men we'd become before they took off. My personal feeling is that that may be why they don't come home."

"That would make sense," she agreed. "Or, they

were terrified of having to do all that shopping at Christmas."

After giving her hand a final squeeze, he reluctantly let it fall to the console separating them. "It's getting expensive," Chandler acknowledged. "But it's been great these past few years. There's something about little kids and Christmas that just warms your heart." He parked in front of the house and cut the engine.

"You softie," she teased, poking a finger at his ribs as they walked up the steps. "Who knew that underneath all this muscle would be a tender, gentle heart."

"I'm showing you my sensitive side and you're ragging me, Dr. Jameson. That's a little harsh, don't you think?"

"Harsh? Yes. But it's also fun."

"I'll show you fun." He scooped her up and smothered her laughter with a deep, meaningful kiss.

In no time her laughter vanished, replaced by spinning, greedy need that left her hanging on to his neck as he explored her mouth and ignited her passions.

Molly was vaguely aware of the sensation of climbing a second flight of stairs. She didn't care all that much; it felt too wonderful to be in his arms, pressed against his powerful body.

Feeling a fleeting sense of impropriety, she halfheartedly said, "We want different things," she suggested.

"We've never talked about what we wanted," he countered, his voice rising a notch. "We can do that, Molly. Later," he said as he cradled her against his solid chest.

Chandler carried her down the hall to his bedroom. As if she were some fragile object, he placed her on the bed, gently arranging her against the pillows.

The lump of emotion threatened to strangle her as the moments of silence dragged on. Molly remained quiet as she watched him shrug out of his shirt before joining her on the bed. Through passion-dilated eyes, she took in the impressive sight of him. Rolling on his side, Chandler pulled her closer, until she encountered the solid outline of his body. His expression was fixed, his mouth little more than a taut line.

"I'll make it good, Molly. You'll see," he said as he gently pulled her into the circle of his arms.

She had no doubt. This felt simply right. She needed this, needed his strength if she was going to make it through this without losing her mind.

She surrendered to the promise she felt in his touch.

Cradling her in one arm, Chandler used his free hand to stroke the hair away from her face. She greedily drank in the scent of his cologne as she cautiously allowed her fingers to rest against his thigh. His skin was warm and smooth, a startling contrast to the very defined muscle she could feel beneath her hand. She remained perfectly still, comforted by his scent, his touch and his nearness. Strange that she could only find such solace in his arms. Being here in this room with Chandler was enough to erase the fear and uncertainty that had plagued her for days. What could be the harm in just a few hours of the pleasure she knew she could find here?

"Molly?" he asked on a strained breath. He captured her face in his hands. His callused thumbs teased her cheekbones. When his chocolate eyes met and held hers, his jaw was set, his expression serious. "I don't know if I have the strength to let you get up and walk away from me now. Please tell me this is what you want. Please?"

Using his hands, he tilted her head back. His face was mere fractions of an inch from hers. She could feel the ragged expulsion of his breath. Instinctively, her palms flattened against his chest. The thick mat of dark hair served as a cushion for her touch. Still, beneath the softness, she could easily feel the hard outline of muscle.

"I want you so badly," he said in a near whisper.

Her lashes fluttered as his words washed over her upturned face. She needed to hear those words, perhaps even wished for them. Chandler's lips tentatively brushed hers. So featherlight was the kiss that she wasn't even certain it could qualify as such. His movements were careful, measured. His thumbs stroked the hollows of her cheeks.

Molly banished all thought from her mind. She wanted this, almost desperately. The touch of his hands and his lips made her feel alive. The ache in her chest was changing, evolving. The fear and confusion were being taken over by some new emotions. She became acutely aware of every aspect of him. The pressure of his thigh where it touched hers. The sound of his uneven breathing. The magical sensation of his mouth on hers.

When he lifted his head, Molly grabbed his broad shoulders. "Don't," she whispered, urging him back to her.

His resistance was both surprising and short-lived. It was almost totally forgotten when he dipped his head. His lips did more than brush against hers. His hands left her face and wound around her slender body. Chandler crushed her against him. She could actually feel the pounding of his heart beneath her hands.

The encounter quickly turned intense and consuming. His tongue moistened her slightly parted lips. The kiss became demanding, with her a very willing participant. She managed to work her hands across his chest until she felt the outline of his erect nipples beneath her palms. He responded to her action by running his hands all over her back and nibbling her lower lip. It was a purely erotic action, inspiring great need and desire in Molly.

A small moan escaped her lips as she kneaded the muscles of his chest. He tasted vaguely of coffee, and he continued to work magic with his mouth. Molly felt the kiss in the pit of her stomach. What had started as a pleasant warmth had grown into a full-fledged heat emanating from her very core, fueled by the sensation of his fingers snaking up her back, entwining in her hair and guiding her head back at a severe angle. Passion flared as he hungrily devoured first her mouth, then the tender flesh at the base of her throat. His mouth was hot, the stubble of his beard slightly abrasive. And she felt it all. She was aware of everything—the outline of his body, the almost arrogant expectation in his kiss. Chandler was obviously a skilled and talented lover. Molly, a compliant and demanding partner.

This was a wondrous new place for her, special and beautiful. The controlled urgency of his need was a heady thing. It gave Molly the sense that she had a certain primal power over this man.

Chandler made quick work of her clothes. He kissed, touched and tasted until Molly literally cried out for their joining. It was no longer an act, it was a need. She needed Chandler inside of her to feel complete.

Poised above her, his brow glistening with perspiration, Chandler looked down at her with smoldering, heavy-lidded eyes. He waited for her to guide him, then filled her with one long, powerful thrust.

The sights and sounds around her became a blur as the knot in her stomach wound tighter with each passing minute, building fiercely until she felt the spasm of satisfaction begin to rack her body. Chandler groaned against her ear as he joined her in release.

As her heart rate returned to normal, her mind was anything but. She lay there perfectly still, not sure what to do or say. She'd made love to Chandler with total and complete abandon. The experience was primitive and wildly scary. Her eyes fluttered in the darkness as she began to think of the consequences for her rash behavior.

Guilt swept over her like a blanket as she realized the gravity of the situation. Things would never be the same between them.

"Where are you going?" Chandler asked as he struggled against her attempt to move out of his arms.

"Back to my room," she suggested.

"No way," he growled sensually as he brushed his lips against her dampened forehead. "I'm not nearly finished making love to you."

"Really?"

Chandler's sigh was loud and meaningful. "You aren't having an attack of second thoughts, are you?"

Placing her hand beneath her cheek, she nodded against his chest. "Um," she mumbled.

"Why?"

"I'm not good at this sort of thing. I don't make a habit of jumping into the sack with a guy just because—"

"Hush," he interrupted. "I know exactly why we made love."

"You do?" She held her breath, scared. "Then tell me because now I'm *totally* confused."

Chapter Fifteen

When Chandler didn't answer right away, she considered tossing herself out the window. Surely that was better than suffering the humiliation of after-spontaneous-sex, stilted, awkward conversation.

"Your silence is deafening," she said when she couldn't stand it another blasted second.

"I'm fairly sure there's something I should have told you before now."

Oh, God! Oh, no. Not the I-really-like-you-but-I'm-not-looking-for-a-serious-relationship-right-now pep talk. That was worse than silence.

"Please." She ripped the blanket from the bed, "don't." She spun to wrap herself in the yards of fabric. "Say." She held the edge of the blanket and snapped up her clothing as she headed for the door. "Another." She stumbled, reaching for her panties, which had somehow landed near the back of his nightstand. "Word."

"Stupid, stupid, stupid," she muttered as soon as

she was safely locked in her own room. Allowing the blanket to fall to the floor, she went into the bathroom and ran the shower. Stepping under the stream, she realized it wouldn't help.

Stupid didn't wash off.

"Physician, heal thyself," she grumbled before the warm water drowned out the sound of her own voice.

AN HOUR LATER Chandler was slamming cabinet doors for no particular reason. Unless he acknowledged that he couldn't think of a single reason why she wouldn't hate the sight of him by morning.

"I know why we made love," he mimicked, his tone heavy with sarcasm and self-disgust. He'd actually meant to say he knew why he'd made love to her. What he didn't know was why he hadn't told her the most important detail of his life beforehand.

"We made love?" Shane asked as he slipped into the room.

Startled and angry at himself, Chandler dropped his beer. Foam and brew sprayed him as a final, crowning insult.

"Not now, Shane."

His younger brother whistled. "I take it that it didn't go well." Shane's expression registered shock and horror. "It did...*go,* though, right?

Chandler grabbed the towel from the handle of the fridge and began sopping up the mess. "When

I said I didn't want to talk, that included my sex life."

"Don't take it out on me," Shane tossed, holding his hands up in surrender while his eyes followed every move Chandler made.

It was annoying. Okay, so maybe deep down inside—way down—he knew his annoyance wasn't directed specifically at Shane. He just happened to be handy.

"Want a beer?"

"In a bottle or do I have to lick it off the floor?"

Chandler paused and leaned over the open door, feeling the cold air rush out and slip between the open edges of the shirt he'd yanked on. He glared at his brother, who didn't so much as flinch. "Do you want one or not?"

"Absolutely," Shane replied. "Can't let you drink alone during your time of crisis."

"You're a regular prince," Chandler drawled, placing two bottles on the table before swinging his leg over the back of his chair, then settling in.

"I hate to break this to you, Chandler," Shane began, stopping long enough to pry the top off both bottles by levering them against the table's edge. "But you aren't your usual chipper self just now. Nothing else happened with John, did it?"

"I don't need John. Apparently I'm very capable of slitting my own wrists."

"What happened?" Shane asked, leaning forward on his elbows and keeping his voice low.

Chandler appreciated the gesture. And, what the hell? Maybe he needed a fresh perspective. "I haven't been totally honest with Molly."

"About what?" Shane challenged. "You're okay on the big one."

"The big one?"

"You aren't otherwise attached to anyone at the moment."

Somehow Chandler didn't find great comfort in that. "There was something I should have told her and didn't."

"So, tell her now."

"It's not that easy," Chandler groaned before taking a long swallow of the bitter drink. "It started out as a private joke. I was amusing myself about this thing at her expense. It wasn't intentional. I didn't plan on feeling this way about her."

"And what way is that?"

Ignoring his brother's irritating and childishly bobbing eyebrows, he answered, "I'm not sure. By the way, that's part two of this problem. I should have thought first and acted second."

"We're men," Shane sang. "We're genetically incapable of thinking before we act when it comes to women."

"That's crap."

"True, but I'm sticking with it, anyway."

"Shane, you aren't helping here."

His brother let out a breath and his expression grew more serious. "Fine. Look, if you aren't willing to come clean with the lady about…whatever, then keep your fly zipped. And if you know in your heart that you should not have gone to bed with the fetching Dr. Jameson, then apologize and mean it."

"She won't be thrilled with either of those possibilities. Is there another option?"

"Sure, you can wait for Taylor to find out you hosed her friend, and your problem will be solved."

His spirits lifted marginally. "Taylor will help me?"

"Nope. She'll kill you, which pretty much makes everything else irrelevant."

"I'M STANDING OUTSIDE NOW," Molly explained. "Can you hear me?"

"I have been worried sick," Claire complained. "I've been reading the papers and watching the news and—wait! First, tell me why hunky news guy isn't on television anymore. What happened? There's a redhead on instead and I promise you, he isn't nearly as much fun to watch as your new friend."

"Hush," Molly pleaded. "I'll tell you if you'll stop talking for a minute."

"Sorry."

"Me, too," Molly admitted, brushing the hair out of her eyes. "I'm going out of my mind."

"John?"

"Chandler. We had a...a thing, and well, that was two days ago and he's practically gone into hibernation since then. He arranged for a deputy to baby-sit here while he goes off to wherever. I'm so bored I could scream."

"You had a *thing?*"

"We're focusing on the boredom," Molly reminded her dearest friend as gently and firmly as possible.

"I'm not bored now. I want to know about the thing."

"This wasn't a good idea."

"Okay, okay," Claire relented. "I'll stop. So long as you promise that exactly one year from now you'll tell me the whole story. Bring pictures if you have any."

"You are so bad."

"No, but apparently you were. So you've been banished to the sticks?"

"It's lovely here, but I need something to *do.*"

"So go to your office and look at some ink blots or whatever it is you do. Take the deputy with you," Claire insisted. "Since John hasn't bothered you in a few days, I think you deserve some early-release time. Just stay with the officer and don't take any unnecessary risks."

"Think that would be okay?"

"Well." Claire paused briefly, then finished by

saying, "I think you're safest right there on the ranch, but I know you. I think so long as you take every possible precaution, you should be able to go to your own office."

"Me, too," she agreed, already feeling better. "I can't see patients, but I can go back through my files to see if I can figure out who John really is."

"But no heroics, right?"

Molly was touched by her friend's concern. "I won't use any of my superpowers on the evildoers. Besides, doesn't it make more sense to think John is just toying with me but his real target is Chandler?" Molly felt dread settle in her stomach when she voiced her hypothesis to Claire. "He's more obvious, and we haven't heard a thing from John since Chandler stopped doing the news."

"That does make sense," Claire agreed. "Want me to do a background check on Chandler? See if anything pops up?"

"Nothing will," Molly insisted. "This family doesn't have secrets. They have the opposite of secrets. I'm guessing none of them are flashy about money because the real currency in this family is privacy."

"Are you picking them apart because you're jealous?"

"Yes," Molly admitted. "I've been trying to hate them, but the truth is, they are the nicest people I've ever met. I'm pretty much a stranger, they've gone out of their way to make me feel welcome. If one isn't making me a home-cooked meal, someone else is sending over a magazine or a book. The phone rings constantly. Someone is always checking on me."

"That is nice," Claire agreed. "You're welcome to come up here, you know."

"I know. I don't want to put you or Stan in danger."

"I love you. We can figure something out if you change your mind."

Molly flicked at a pebble with her big toe, truly touched by her friend's willingness to sacrifice. But she wouldn't change her mind. "I'm good," she insisted. "Gavin offered to let me crash at his place. I told him no, as well."

"Really? Liking life as a Landry, huh?"

Just liking one Landry in particular, she thought. "Worse things could happen to you."

"Are you sure there's nothing I can do? I'm a computer genius, Mol. Let me hack into a few secure servers on your behalf just to check on the Landry brothers. If there's any gossip to be—"

"No." Molly was emphatic. Aside from knowing it was futile, there was something inappropriate about gathering information about Chandler and his family that she had no business knowing. Chandler had been very open and honest from the get-go, and she didn't have a hope in hell of sorting out their relationship if she did something so desperately under-handed.

Relationship. The word played in her mind long after she'd said goodbye to Claire. They didn't have a relationship, they had a…a what?

Nothing. Especially if she couldn't get Chandler to say more than polite niceties.

"Why does it have to be so hard?" she asked as she went in search of the deputy to let him know about their road trip.

He was less than enthusiastic.

"I have orders, ma'am. Orders from the sheriff."

"Then why don't I just call the sheriff," she suggested.

Molly returned to the house, grabbed the phone from its cradle and pounded the numbers on the keypad in the order supplied on a sheet of paper in what she now recognized as Chandler's neat, block printing.

Seth's secretary put her through almost immediately. "Hi, Molly, is there a problem?"

"Want them in random or chronological order?"

"You don't sound happy," he said, his voice calm, reasonable and tinged with an appropriate amount of concern. "What happened?"

"I'm tired of house arrest," she grumbled without preamble. "I want to go to my office, but the teenage brown shirt you have posted at the door won't cooperate."

She heard him muffle a laugh before saying, "He's almost thirty."

"Whatever. Look, Chandler gets to go off all day. Why am I cooped up and guarded like a terrorist?"

"For your own safety?" She heard him expel a breath. "I'm sure its getting to you, but I think you should hang on a bit longer."

"No. I heard you talking to Chandler last night. I know you've had my office under surveillance twenty-four hours a day since John left the bomb there for poor Mr. LaBrett to find. I need to go there, Seth. I still haven't gone through my patient files. It has to be done."

"I'll do it."

"No way," she insisted. "They're confidential medical records."

"I don't like the idea of you going alone. Can't you wait for Chandler to finish his…to finish?"

His what? Too bad she wasn't a real Landry. They didn't have secrets between them, and she'd have some idea where he was and what he was up to. Thus far she'd gotten little more than vague claims about working on *something*.

"No, Seth. Even if I have to call old Moe at the filling station to ask for a ride in his tow truck, I'm going to my office."

"I'll radio the deputy," Seth relented, though she could tell he wasn't happy about it. "He'll drive you and stay with you."

"Fine."

"I mean *stay* with you, Molly. Not outside, not in the next room, I mean in plain sight at all times."

Touched by his very genuine concern for her safety, Molly thanked him. "I'll be good, promise."

"Will you do me a favor?"

"Sure."

"When you get to your office, will you give me a call?"

"I have to check in?"

"Yes. But I also need whatever nonconfidential information you have on Jonas Black. I'm still not finding anything current on him."

She agreed, though she was certain that Seth was barking up the wrong tree. Jonas and John were not one and the same.

It was an unusually warm day by Montana standards so she ran up and changed from slacks to a pair of shorts and a trendy T-shirt she'd borrowed with Taylor's permission. The clothing she'd bought didn't even come close to rebuilding a wardrobe.

Besides, this outfit was far more suited to rummaging around in the basement, searching dusty old files.

Deputy pencil neck drove her into town, passed the park where normal people were. Doing normal things like playing ball, sharing picnics and jogging the path that ran parallel to the road. It was a beautiful, sunny day and she was going to spend it stuck inside.

Well, if she was going to be a prisoner of necessity, she was going to make good use of her confinement. After making that decision, she felt as if a weight had been lifted from her shoulders. Until and if something else happened, she vowed not to let her fear of John control her anymore.

And the same for Chandler. Well, not the same. John's actions toyed with her mind. Chandler had a direct line to her heart. That was a harder war to wage.

And a stupid one, to boot. They were both adults. So what if they had one lapse in judgment? This cold war was childish and she wasn't interested in letting it continue. The next time she saw Chandler, she would simply clear the air. Let him know that while it had been a pleasant diversion, she was fine with it being nothing more than that.

Okay, so fine was a stretch. Odd as it seemed, she *could* be fine with it. Especially if that meant they could go back to being friends. She missed him. Molly would rather have him be *in* her life than a memory *from* her life.

Okay, if she suddenly got complete control over the universe, Chandler would be more than her friend. At the very least, he'd be adult enough and brave enough to just see what might happen.

"Men are such jerks," she muttered.

"I'm sorry, ma'am, I didn't hear you."

Just as well. She'd all but forgotten about the deputy during the drive. "It's up ahead on the right," she said as the entrance to the parking lot came into view.

A few minutes later she was inside, with the deputy on her heels, the strap on his holster unsnapped. The heavy scent of industrial cleaner almost smacked her in the face. Then she was hit again by the memory of finding her patient dead. Everything in the room was spotless. The only indication that a brutal murder had occurred was a very faint stain next to the waiting-room chair. Bypassing that section, she moved to the second door and used her key.

Crooking her finger, she said, "C'mon. Follow me." She showed him into the private office, tossing her keys and her purse on the cluttered desk, then moving to the double doors to open them, as well. "There's soda and water in the minifridge. Probably a few candy bars in there, too."

She turned to find him standing like a statue in the center of the room. This isn't going to work. Donning her brightest smile, she asked, "Do you have a first name?"

"Ma'am?"

"A name? Surely your parents didn't call you Deputy."

He blushed and grinned all at once. "No, ma'am. Riggs. Harlen Riggs."

"May I call you Harlen?"

The color on his cheeks deepened. "Bud, ma'am. I go by Bud."

Who knew it took twenty questions to end up with Bud? "Okay, Bud. Call me Molly. I'm going to work now, so you can do…whatever it is you do. That door—" she paused and pointed to a small door nearly hidden by the large chair angled out from the corner "—that leads down to the basement. I might have to go downstairs in a little while."

"I'll be going with you, ma'am. Sheriff was real clear on that."

She shrugged and went to her chair, falling into it, then scooting over to the first of three file drawers.

It was one of those situations where she didn't know what she was looking for but hoped she'd recognize it when she saw it. She'd call Seth when and *if* she did. Though she couldn't hold the proverbial candle to Chandler's pathological penchant for organization, she started in the most logical place. The green folders. They were the court-ordered cases dating back two years.

Absently she tapped the eraser end of her pencil on the desktop as she read through the files. All the *A*s, then the *B*s, and so on and so on. She reached the letter *F* before the need to stand and stretch took hold.

Deputy Riggs reminded her of those dedicated

soldiers she saw on the television. The ones who stood guard over national monuments. Eyes straight ahead, alert and as stiff as a statue. "Want something to drink?"

On her way to the minifridge, she stopped, placed her hands at her waist and bent from side to side in an attempt to loosen the tight muscles at the small of her back.

"Anything would be fine, ma'am."

She grabbed two bottles of water and handed one off to him. "Do you want a magazine or something?"

"I'm fine, ma'am."

After taking a drink, she jumped to sit up on her desk and regarded him for part of a minute. "This is me taking a break," she explained. "Live a little, Bud. At least take your hat off."

Somewhat reluctantly he removed the standard-issue Stetson and placed it gently in his lap. It was a start. "So, when you're not baby-sitting me, what kinds of things do you like?"

"Ma'am?"

She rolled her eyes. "I'll give you a hundred bucks if you'll stop calling me that. Molly is fine. Really."

"Yes, Ma— Molly."

"We're making great headway," she told him, ignoring the wary look in his pale eyes. "How long have you been with the sheriff's department?"

"Going on five years."

"Do you like it?"

Some of the trepidation drained from his expression. "Yes. Yes, I do. I get to help people. I meet a lot of interesting people in my line of work."

"Did you always want to be a cop?"

He nodded, giving her a glimpse of scalp through the closely shorn stubble on his head. "Since I was small. My daddy was in the military. An MP. I thought about the service, but it wasn't really for me."

"Me, neither."

There was a long, painful gap in their fragmented attempt at conversation. Molly had pretty much given up on him when he suddenly asked, "Are you a real doctor?"

The temptation to point to the degrees framed on the wall behind her was strong, but she opted not to, instead telling him about her training. "I even spent three months at Quantico working with their Behavioral Science Unit."

"Like in *Silence of the Lambs?*" He perked right up then.

"Yes. I learned all about profiling criminals. It was pretty interesting. I liked the—" Her cell phone rang at the same time someone began pounding on the front door.

Concurrent events seemed to throw her protector into a state of confusion. Gently she suggested, "You get the door while I answer my phone."

As if her cell service wasn't already a challenge, she heard Chandler's voice bellowing through the office just as she was trying to navigate around the room in search of a clear signal. "Hello?"

Static.

"Dammit! Hello? Hang on," she walked out into the waiting room. "Are you still there?"

"Hel...olly...ollege" was all she was able to catch from the garbled connection.

"Gavin?" she yelled, pushing past Chandler—though mentally noting he looked quite handsome—to reach the outside. "Gavin? Is that you?"

"Molly, dear," Gavin began in a rush, "something dreadful has happened."

Chapter Sixteen

"Gavin? What is it?"

"It's Rachel, I'm afraid," he said. "I just arrived at the departmental offices and, well, she was stabbed. They've taken her to the hospital, but the prognosis isn't good."

"What can I do?"

"Hang up," Chandler said, taking the phone from her and flipping it closed. "We've got to go."

She glared up at him through teary eyes. "My teaching assistant—"

"Was attacked," he finished. "That's why I'm here. We're getting you the hell out of here. Now."

"But—"

Ignoring her protestations—which were echoed in vain by the officer—he gripped her arm and quickly led her to the still-idling SUV. He could have been a little more gentle, but just then all he could think of was getting her to Seth's office. It was the closest absolutely safe place.

"Why are you here?"

"Seth called me."

"My TA is attacked and he called you? Why not Harlen?"

"Harlen?" he repeated as he peeled out of the parking lot fast enough to fill the car with the acrid smell of burning rubber.

"My deputy."

"You're on a first-name basis with him?" He glanced over and was surprised to see a single tear slipping down her cheek. He slammed the heel of his hand against the wheel. He took in two slow, calming gulps of air and hated himself for the poor way he'd handled this. Not just this. Everything. But that could wait. Right now he had to stay focused. And part of that focus had to include common decency. He divided his attention between the road and dabbing the tear from her cheek.

Chandler felt his chest tighten as a second tear spilled forth. He swerved to the curb and threw the gearshift into Park. "Come here," he instructed softly.

"Gavin said it was bad."

"It is," Chandler said, releasing the seat belt and lifting her over the console. "But there's hope." Which was true. Slim hope, but hope. He stroked her hair as he kissed her forehead while the blue and red flashing emergency lights from the deputy's cruiser strobed from behind.

"Why Rachel?" Molly asked, her voice trembling.

"Who knows."

"It was John?"

"Mmm-hmm."

"What aren't you telling me?"

He didn't want to tell her. He really didn't. But she deserved to know. "Thirteen stab wounds."

"Oh, no!" Molly cried, burying her face against him.

He held her fragile form until he no longer felt the shudders of her silent agony. She went still but didn't make any move to get away from him.

She should have. His behavior these past few days was inexcusable. That realization had come to him moments before hearing of Rachel's probably fatal attack. He'd been at his desk at home, typing the same flawed sentence for the hundredth time when he finally felt ready to face reality.

It made no sense. It went against everything he'd ever felt or believed. But it was true. He knew that with every fiber of his being.

Chandler continued to stroke her hair as he stared blindly out the window. It shouldn't have happened. It wasn't supposed to happen. Not like this. Not in a matter of days. Hours, really. But it had. He'd fallen in love with her just that quickly. And try as he might—and he had—to ignore it or dismiss it, it wasn't to be.

He had finally come to terms with his feelings and was planning a way to tell her when Seth had called. The news about Rachel was surprising. She seemed an unlikely victim, given that Molly hadn't set foot on the campus since the day John first called the station.

It was nothing compared to the shocking news delivered by Seth that Molly wasn't safely back at the ranch. Instead she'd somehow convinced Seth to let her go to her office.

Battling panic the whole way, Chandler had made record time getting to her. Though he knew the timing wasn't right to admit his feelings, he'd wanted to be the one to tell her about Rachel.

She roused slowly, wiping her face with the backs of her hands. Reading the pain in those big green eyes felt like someone had sliced his heart in two. Tucking her hair behind her ear, he leaned forward to brush his lips to hers.

"W-why did Seth call you and not me?" she asked, tugging at the hem of her shirt before shifting back into the passenger's seat.

"He was about to call you, but I wanted to. I thought it was better if you heard it from a friend."

Her head tilted to one side. "When did you decide we were friends?"

He touched the pad of his forefinger to her lips. "Hush. This isn't the time for this conversation. Let's just say that I know I owe you a huge apology for being such an ass since we—"

"I understand," she insisted. "And you're right. This isn't the time or—" she glanced around "—the place."

"Let's go to Seth's office."

"Will he be there?"

Chandler thought for a second, then shook his head. "I'm sure he's gone out to the college. Technically they have jurisdiction, but I don't think anyone on the security force can spell murder, let alone investigate one."

"She isn't dead yet."

He cringed. "Sorry. You've got to brace yourself for that possibility, Molly. Her injuries were substantial."

"Then let's go back to my office."

"What?"

"I'm going through my files looking for some clue to John's identity. I can't go to the hospital because I'm sure once news of Rachel's attack and its link to John gets out, the place will be crawling with reporters."

He saw the faint stain of color on her cheeks and it curved the very corners of his mouth.

"Sorry. No offense intended."

"None taken. Besides, I'm a *former* reporter."

"And we both know that John seems to be more active when you or I show up on television, so we should avoid any kind of exposure."

"Agreed." It felt good to be with her again. Really with her. He'd missed the soft lilt of her voice and kind intelligence in her eyes. Hell, he missed everything. When this was over he'd make it all right again. Assuming he could. Chandler swallowed, unwilling to acknowledge the lump of fear that threatened to block his throat when he so much as considered speculating on what her reaction might be. What her feelings might be.

"I think there's something in the files," she said. "I'm not sure what, but my intuition tells me it's worth looking for."

"Good plan," he agreed, making a U-turn and heading back with the deputy shadowing them. "Besides, it will pass the time. Rachel will go directly into surgery. It could be hours before we find out anything."

"I'm not comfortable with you looking through my files," she said apologetically.

"No problem." He pointed his thumb in the direction of the backseat. "I've got my laptop with me. I can keep myself occupied."

"Doing what?"

Pretending to check the side mirror, he avoided her gaze, then answered, "I can play games, plug in and surf porn sites, or—ouch!" He rubbed the sore spot on his bicep where she'd poked him with her fingernail.

"Porn sites? That's vile."

He shot her a lecherous grin. "And you know that how?"

"One time, by accident, I opened an e-mail and—"

"Visited hundreds of hot coeds?"

Her smile stole his breath. "No. The e-mail's subject line simply read 'I need your help,' so, assuming it was from a patient, I opened it."

"How long did it take you to get over the shock?"

"I wasn't shocked," she insisted, all proper and businesslike. "I was disgusted. There's a huge difference between sexuality and trafficking in images that are degrading and demeaning to women. Porn, in case you're confused, is the latter."

"Porn does not confuse me," he deadpanned.

She leaned close to him as he parked the car in front of her office complex. "If you're really bored, you can try to drag some conversation out of Harlen."

"Harlen is on his own," Chandler promised. "I'll call Seth and tell him where we are, then I'm going to work. You won't even know I'm here."

Fat chance. Not when her heart was racing and a good strain of anticipation settled in the pit of her stomach as she drank in the familiar, comforting scent of him.

She was thrilled to have him with her. More than she should have been, more than was safe, but she didn't care. Molly knew absolutely that she was happier, more contented, more alive when she was with Chandler. So long as she avoided any verbal dissection of their nonrelationship, she could be happy in her pretend bliss.

True to his word, Chandler called Seth from the outer office. Molly liked hearing the deep resonance of his voice as she dove back in to the files. It was comforting and exciting and purely male in cadence.

Having him there made it a challenge to concentrate, but it was a trade she willingly made.

A few minutes later he appeared in the doorway, his fancy laptop tucked under his arm. "Rachel is still hanging on," he reported. "Where do you want me?"

Good for Rachel and...I want you naked on the floor. "I'm spread out all over the place, so anyplace that's convenient for you is fine. Do you need to plug in your computer?"

"Not yet," he replied, grabbing a spot on the couch and stuffing a pillow under his head. He balanced the computer on his stomach, his fingers flying across the keypad.

Molly was impressed. She was one of those poor souls who had never mastered the art of typing. She was a hunt-and-peck person, with just enough dexterity to draft her thumb into service on the spacebar.

She was skimming through Alan Gastler's file for the third time when she spotted a notation she'd made regarding his religious practices. "You get bar-mitzvahed at age thirteen. Maybe John has some sort of religious theme going on."

She stood and pulled her copy of the Bible from the bookcase. A quick check confirmed her belief. The thirteenth books of the Old and New Testaments didn't have the kind of imagery that a typical unstable mind might latch on to. So much for that idea.

She diligently continued to pore over the notes and records, stopping occasionally to get a drink, stretch or simply admire Chandler. A very pleasant diversion. Fixed on his task, he didn't notice as her gaze roamed openly along his long, lean frame. Desire sang in her core as she admired his powerful thighs, broad chest and sculpted profile. The man simply made her weak in the knees.

He, however, seemed amazingly immune. It was like he was in his own world. Whatever he was doing, it had his full, undivided attention. Molly was pretty sure she could strip naked and he wouldn't notice.

While knowing that didn't do much for her feminine sensibilities, she thought, adding dedication to the growing list of things she respected about him.

She'd reviewed and discarded three more files when his cell phone rang. Looking up, she wondered if the sound would penetrate his deep concentration. It did. Eventually.

Snapping it off the clip at his belt, he pressed it

to his ear and growled, "What? We are. I don't know, hang on." He looked over at Molly, holding the phone away from his chiseled mouth. "Is the phone out? Seth says he's been calling for a while."

She shook her head. "It won't ring here. I set it to automatically transfer calls to my home phone. But my home got blown up and I don't know how to cancel the bypass."

"Did you get that?" he asked into the cell.

He continued his call. Apparently he had better quality service. She made a mental note to call someone to fix her telephone woes. There were undoubtedly messages awaiting her reply trapped in the system, hopefully none were of an emergency nature.

"You're breaking up," Chandler yelled, placing the laptop on the carpet as he rose. "Hang on, I'm walking outside."

The scent of his cologne lingered in the room. It was impossible to think about John when her brain was so totally engrossed with her secret longings for Chandler. Well, not so secret, she acknowledged.

Taking her next break, she was surprised that Chandler was still on the phone with Seth. She stepped over his laptop on her way to the minifridge. On her return, she weakened. Though it went against everything she believed in, she just couldn't help herself. Not when the screen was big and the words were right there in front of her. It wasn't as if she'd intended to snoop, it was more like taking advantage of a situation when presented.

"...lots of bombs explode. The hero links an attractive thief to a terrorist cell to Switzerland the thief has stolen important data from."

"I can explain," Chandler began, looking at her with total panic in his dark eyes upon his return.

She offered her best smile. "You don't have to explain. I think it's great."

Deep furrows wrinkled his brow. "You do?"

She nodded enthusiastically. "Of course I do." She patted the cushion next to hers, inviting him to join her. The man continued to surprise her. "It's your book, right?"

"Just a rough synopsis." He seemed tense as he sat down.

She guessed at the reason for his discomfort. "Scary, isn't it?"

"Not really."

She wasn't buying it. Everyone got a little scared when they tried a new thing. Writers, at least the ones she knew, were an insecure group. They needed a lot of praise, and she'd seen some pretty successful people dissolve into tears, all because of a form rejection letter or a bad review.

"I only glanced at a few lines, but it seems you're off to a strong start."

He smiled almost shyly. "You aren't exactly an impartial judge. I already know you like me."

Well, that was one way of putting it. Not *her* way, but she'd let that pass for now. "I did see a couple of potential problem areas, though."

"Such as?"

She took his hands in hers and held them. "The plot doesn't feel...fresh."

"Really?"

It was important to her that she give him useful, constructive criticism without dashing his obvious enthusiasm. "It's a little overdone," she explained. "I get several publishing industry e-mail alerts, and it seems that every Tom, Dick and Jane is writing action/adventure with a romantic twist."

"It is a popular subgenre."

"And very specific. The readers have expectations, Chandler. You never get a second chance to disappoint them. May I make a suggestion?"

"Shoot?"

"I'd be willing to call my agent on your behalf. Once you have your synopsis and the first few chapters together, then—"

"Molly?" he began, braced for any reaction but realistically expecting the worst.

She smiled sweetly. "Don't say it. I know you think it's an imposition and that I could possibly get the idea that you've only been nice to me just to get me to hook you up with my contacts. I don't want—"

"My mother's name was Priscilla Connor."

She blinked twice in rapid succession. He could tell she still wasn't putting it together.

"My family owns the Lucky 7 Ranch. Seth and Savannah gave their son *her* family name. If you—"

"Wait!" she yelped, her eyes darted around.

He could almost see her fitting the pieces into place.

She gaped up at him. Her mouth opened as if she was about to say something. There was another long, tense silence, then she looked down at his hands as if she didn't know what they were.

"Lucky 7. S-E-V-E-N. L for Lucky. S for seven. Your mother…oh, my gosh! L. S. Connor!" Her gaze lifted slowly until her eyes locked on his. "You're L. S. Connor? You're him?"

He nodded. "I know you're furious, because I should have told you. But I had no idea we would—"

She flung her arms around his neck and squeezed so tightly he was afraid he might black out from the lack of oxygen. "You're L. S. Connor. How cool is that?"

"You aren't mad?" he asked after he gently pried her arms from his throat.

"Mad? I'm astounded. I…I mean I'm a huge fan of his—yours. So is most of the rest of the world. But…wow. This is *so* cool."

"I thought you might—" He was cut off by the revival of his cell phone. Cursing softly, he yanked it to his ear and said, "Hello?" Then, "Wait! I can't hear you."

She stared at his back as he took the frustrated walk outside, still stunned at the news. Chandler Landry was L .S. Connor. Of course he was. It made perfect sense. No wonder she'd fallen for him in record time. Through his writing, she'd known him for years.

Chandler came rushing back into the room, his expression grim. "Seth found Jonas Black."

"Where?"

"The hospital."

"Is he hurt?"

"No." Chandler scowled and looked as if he might explode. "But he will be soon."

Chapter Seventeen

"Let me make sure I understand this," Molly said. "Jonas Black is Rachel's brother?"

"Stepbrother," Chandler corrected as he paced the small confines of her office. "Which explains how he got so much information about you. Rachel must have been feeding it to him all along."

Molly tried to process this development. He was right, it did make sense. It explained a lot. *If* she believed that Rachel was somehow involved in the murders and bombings. "If Rachel was helping Jonas, why was she attacked?"

Chandler shrugged. "Who knows. Maybe she and Jonas had a falling out? You tell me. You know them both."

"I do," Molly agreed, twirling a lock of hair around her finger. "Frankly, I can't see either one of them doing all this. Rachel is a sweet young woman—girl really—who would never hurt anyone." She grabbed a handful of his sleeve and looked up into his eyes. "Think about the first crime," she argued. "Do we know for a fact that the branded torso is Rachel's mother?"

Chandler picked up on her suggestion. "Should be easy enough to check. I'm going to meet Seth. I want to be there when he questions Jonas. Will you be okay?"

No. "Sure."

He started for the door, turned and then came back and pulled her into his arms. His kiss was slow and thoughtful. Molly's hands flattened against the strong muscles at his back, slid upward until her hands hooked his shoulders, allowing her to pull him even closer. His tongue darted out, teasing hers as he cupped her face in her hands.

She felt him reluctantly begin to pull away. Moving backward until only their lips touched. "I have to go. I hate it, but I have to," he mumbled against her mouth.

"Maybe I should come with you?" she suggested, feeling abandoned when the kiss ended.

"There are reporters everywhere, but I'll leave the decision up to you."

Sighing heavily, she shook her head. "No. I'll just hang out here. I'm really not in the mood to be jostled and shouted out by a hoard of—"

He touched the tip of his finger to her nose, flashed a killer grin, then winked. "They're just doing their jobs, Molly. This shouldn't take long. I'm really happy that this is just about over."

This *us* or this *John?* She didn't dare ask. It was easier to let him rush out.

"I'm such a chicken," she muttered, returning to her files. "That was classic avoidance."

She wasn't sure she wanted an answer to her question about their future—assuming they might actually have one. Rachel and Jonas were an entirely different matter.

A quick check in the filing cabinet failed to reveal Jonas's file, so she headed downstairs. It was a dank, musty-smelling area that she normally avoided. The air felt cool and clammy against her skin, and she could actually taste the accumulated dust particles.

White file boxes lined the walls. She scanned the labels, finally finding her target on—wouldn't you know it—the bottom of a tall stack.

"And people think psychiatry isn't physically demanding," she joked as she lifted each heavy box and moved it across the room like an ant building a bridge one grain of sand at a time. Ten boxes later she wiped perspiration from her brow before stripping the lid from the box.

Thankfully there was a small window that allowed some daylight into the basement. Aided by a naked bulb hanging from the ceiling, she could just read the names on the folders as she sorted the contents.

"There you are, Jonas," she greeted. Retrieving the folder, she blew a steady stream of breath at it, then tucked it under her arm as she wiped her hands on the backside of her shorts. Taylor's shorts, actually. Oh, well, they'd have to be washed anyway.

Molly spent the next twenty minutes poring over every note, every detail of her sessions with Jonas. On a notepad, she jotted down all the dates Jonas had mentioned his mother during his treatment. There were a total of eleven.

In order to verify her suspicions, Molly grabbed her cell and went out front. She was stuck in the labyrinth of the college's automated phone system when it dawned on her that Deputy Riggs was gone. No deputy. No cruiser. Nothing. The only car in the lot was the sensible sedan she recognized as belonging to Ken Ross, the highly allergic CPA in the next office.

Those few seconds of distraction cost her. She was dropped from the phone system and forced to redial and start from scratch. Seven options later she was put through to the Human Resources Office. "This is Dr. Jameson. Could you pull Rachel Mitchell's application for me?"

"Please hold."

Her foot tapped impatiently as she was forced to listen to canned music. "C'mon, c'mon," she whispered, counting songs while she waited.

"I've got it, Doctor. Rachel Mitchell," she read off

an address Molly recognized as the apartment complex across the street from the college. The woman then asked, "Is there something else you need?"

"What was her mother's name?"

"Nathan. Jeanette Nathan."

"Is there an address?"

"No."

"You're sure?" Molly pressed.

"Positive. According to the paper in my hand, Rachel's mother died several years ago. Is there a problem? She's getting Federal money for her education, and if there's an impropriety on her applica—"

"No," Molly interrupted. "No problem. Thanks for your help." She flipped the phone off without waiting for an acknowledgment.

Scratching her head, she wasn't quite sure what to do. Or how to do it. The absent deputy—where was he anyway?—had left her stranded.

She pressed the memory button and listened to the ring until it was answered by a friendly, familiar voice. "Hi, Gavin, it's Molly."

"Where are you?"

"My office," she answered on a breath. "Listen, you hired Rachel, right?"

"Yes, lovely girl. Honest, earnest. I'm just sick over what's happened to her."

"Me, too."

"If there's an adverse outcome, we will have lost

a promising student as well as a stellar teaching assistant. You've been reading her thesis. What a shame. She was a bright girl."

Who isn't dead yet, Molly thought. Then again, Gavin had found her, so he might know more about the gravity of the situation. "Do you know anything about her? Anything personal?"

"No, why would I? She was assigned to you. Surely you had more personal contact with her than I ever did. Molly, is something the matter? You sound frazzled."

"That's one way of putting it," she managed to say. "Seth and Chandler have found a connection between Rachel and that Jonas guy who was giving me some grief a while back."

"That was unpleasant, as I recall."

"They think he's John."

There was a long pause, then, "Well, good. I know these past few days have been trying for you. Now you will be able to return to your responsibilities here. Your students have missed you and so have I. You belong in the classroom, Molly. Perhaps this most recent event will convince you to make academia your focus again. I worry about you, dear."

"Thanks. And believe me, after this week, the calm, boring world of lectures and grading papers is sounding better and better."

"Just something for you to consider."

She raked her hair off her face. "Think, Gavin. Is

there anything at all about Rachel that seemed strange?"

"I am sorry, my dear, but my answer has not changed in the past minute. I wish I could be of help to you."

"Thanks, anyway."

"How about dinner tonight?"

"Maybe," she hedged. "I want to check something out first."

"Let the authorities do their work, Molly."

"Seth and Chandler are convinced they have their man."

"And you remain suspicious?"

"I'd like something more concrete than guilt by association."

"I am sure that given time, the authorities will develop sufficient evidence to satisfy even you."

She ended the call wondering if maybe her imagination was just getting the best of her. Gavin was probably right. She should wait to see what would happen.

She went back to her office intending to clean up her mess. She began to file away the records when a specific name caught her eye.

Just reading it caused a shiver to dance the full length of her spine. She remembered the cold, lifeless eyes. Her court-assigned patient had come in twice a week for six months. The man oozed anger. Anger toward women. Anger toward minorities. Anger at the government. And anger in general.

"A lot like John," she realized. Only, her former patient had died in a prison fight, so she tossed his file on top of her desk as a new idea began to germinate in her mind.

Molly stepped outside, flipped open her cell phone and noticed the flashing red light above the keypad. "You can *not* be serious!" she wailed, completely tempted to smash the thing on the pavement. "Low battery? Are you kidding me?"

Utterly frustrated, she walked the few steps to Ken's office and opened the door. She smelled medicinal air cleaner as a bell jingled over head. Ken came running out, tissue in hand.

"How are you?" he greeted. "I didn't think you'd be back for a while."

"May I use your phone?" she asked, waving her nearly deceased cell in the air. "My battery is dead and my office lines are…forget it, the explanation isn't important."

Ken led her back to his office. Papers were mounded on three sides, making the small space look more like the inside of an igloo than an office. He stepped over and opened a drawer, pulling out an antibacterial wipe and handing it to her.

Confused, Molly said, "I need to use your phone, not wash your windows."

He made a nervous laughlike sound, then sneezed

twice. "You're welcome to it." He scurried around the desk. "I'll step out to give you some privacy. Just please wipe the phone down when you're through."

She waited until he closed the door before grumbling, "Right, because millions of people die every year from phone cooties." If anything, *she* should be the germophobe. Ken sneezed constantly, spewing any number of things she didn't even want to think about.

Dialing the number, she groaned when a mechanical voice came on, giving a list of options available. "Did someone pass a law making it illegal for real people to answer phones?"

When she learned that pressing the *0* would direct her to a hospital operator, she nearly jumped for joy.

"How may I direct your call?"

"I need to speak to Sheriff Landry. It's important."

"Is he on staff here?"

"He's the sheriff," Molly answered, exasperated. "He's probably wherever you've got a patient named Rachel Mitchell."

"I have that patient listed in the system, ma'am. She's still in surgery."

"I know that. The sheriff is somewhere in the hospital."

"I'm not authorized to do general pages. You can try your call later, when the patient is out of surgery."

"Thanks." Molly smashed the button and tried to remember the direct number to Seth's office. She couldn't, so she opted to use 911. It was immediately answered by a calm, male attendant.

"What is your emergency?"

"I need to speak to Sheriff Landry immediately. This is Molly Jameson."

"This is 911, ma'am. If you have an emergency—"

"I need the sheriff. Can't you patch me through to him or something?"

"I can't, ma'am. You can call that office directly on the nonemergency number."

"Which is?" She grabbed a felt-tipped pen off Ken's desk and wrote the numbers on the palm of her hand. Irritation and frustration had her annoyance at an all-time high. All that adrenaline surging through her made Molly perspire, so she swiped her forehead at the same instant she realized what an incredibly stupid thing that was.

Looking down at her palm, she winced when she saw the smear of blurred blue numbers. "I quit," she sighed, slamming the receiver onto the cradle.

Rushing out of the room, she found Ken sitting in his waiting room, dabbing at his nose. He stood, looking almost relieved that she was finished.

"Thanks," she began.

He reached for the doorknob. "Anytime. I'm always happy to help a neighbor."

"Good, because I need to borrow your car."

"My car?" He made it sound like she'd asked for a kidney.

"It's an emergency, Ken."

"My phone is one thing." He managed to get out the last syllable before a sneezing fit. "I don't normally make a habit of lending out my car."

She struggled to keep her tone even. "And I wouldn't dream of imposing under normal circumstances, but as I said, this is an emergency."

Sneeze. Sneeze. Big sneeze. "I read what happened to that newsman's car." Sneeze. "I don't believe my insurance covers explosive devices."

Her patience snapped. Her fists balled and she narrowed her eyes as she stepped just a little closer to him. "I need the keys, Ken. Now." She held her hand palm up in front of his face. "Now, or I swear, I'll go through this entire office and lick everything in sight. Doorknobs, pencil sharpeners. I'll put my germs in places you can't even dream of."

With trembling hands he dug into his pocket and pulled out an leatherette case, reluctantly passing it to Molly.

She accepted, slapping her cell in his hand. "Keep this as collateral."

"My car for a dead phone?"

"Life isn't always fair," she sighed as she sprinted out to his car.

"THE BLOOD TYPES don't match," Seth said after reading from the reports he'd been handed. "We don't even have to wait on the DNA. Jonas and Rachel are definitely not related to the torso."

Chandler's spirits sank. He so wanted it to be Jonas. The knowledge that Molly was still in danger felt like a sucker punch to the gut. Chandler lifted his foot and kicked a chair across the small conference room they'd been given to interview Jonas Black.

"We're back to square one," he grumbled.

"Not necessarily," Seth offered.

Chandler held his breath and listened.

"The crime lab in Helena ran the spec on the bombs. I've got good news and bad news. Which one do you want first?"

"Good news first."

Seth shuffled the papers and said, "The computer found several bombs with the same basic design and construction as the one at Molly's office."

Chandler's interest was piqued. "This is a known bomber?"

"Maybe," Seth hedged. "The bomb at Molly's house and the one that blew your car into itty, bitty pieces was too fragmented for a conclusive match."

"Hell," Chandler sighed, standing with a renewed sense of purpose, "I'll take one out of three if it leads us to this scumbag." He went over and patted his brother's shoulder. "Good work, Seth. And, by the way, I don't think a one-out-of-three match is bad news."

"It wasn't," Seth said. "The bad news is the guy convicted of building that particular kind of bomb is dead."

Chandler hung his head and cursed. "So we pretty much have a ghost building the bombs, an unidentified torso with a thirteen branded on it, a woman who was shot and then stabbed thirteen times, and now a—" Chandler's brain spun, then a tentative smile came to his lips as he experienced his theory with a clarity that came in a sudden, clear flash.

"A what?" Seth asked.

Chandler threw his hands in the air, then let them slap against his thighs. "Thirteen *is* the key. Molly was right."

"I'm still a page behind," Seth prompted.

Excitedly Chandler tested his idea. "I'm guessing that the dead bomber in the computer system was militia?"

He watched as Seth scanned the report in his hands. "It's got to be."

"Thirteen colonies," they said in unity. "Freedom Nation."

"I'm going to tell Molly," Chandler announced.

Seth grabbed his phone and called his office, shouting orders and directions. "I want to know everything about Peter Geller, down to the name of his favorite dog and I want it yesterday. Oh," Seth glanced over at him as he added, "And check with the clerk's office. See if any member of the Geller family ever had court-ordered sessions with Dr. Jameson."

"This has to be it," Chandler shouted, renewed energy cursing through his system.

"Good work, bro."

"Don't thank me yet," Seth cautioned.

They were glad-handing each other when the intercom system blurted out, "Sheriff Landry, please report to postop immediately. Sheriff Landry to postop."

They stopped their celebration. "Think she made it?" Chandler asked, following his brother out into the hallway.

"No. Maybe. I hope so. Taylor called me earlier."

"Really?" Chandler asked.

"Apparently Taylor has had a few classes with Rachel and she wanted me to know I was wrong to suspect her of anything."

"Taylor is a smart woman."

Seth grinned. "She sure is keeping Shane on his toes."

"Molly didn't think Rachel could be involved, either," Chandler offered just as they reached the automatic doors to the critical care area.

Rachel Mitchell was alive. Barely. According to the surgeon, it was nothing short of a miracle. "She's quite agitated," the doctor added. "She kept trying to point at the guard you posted, so we got her a tablet and she wrote this."

He presented them the item. It was hard to read, but good enough for all to agree that she'd managed to form the letter G and a circular shape—an e maybe?—on the paper.

"Does this help in your investigation?"

Chandler could have kissed the guy. The first two letters in Geller's name? "You bet." He turned to Seth and asked, "What are we waiting for?"

"I'll have search and arrest warrants in under an hour. Go call Molly, let her know what's happening."

He didn't need prodding. Even if he didn't have good news, he'd still love to hear the sultry sound of her voice. The fact that an arrest was in the works just made it all that much sweeter.

"...lo?"

Chandler decided that one of the first things he'd do was buy the woman a decent cell phone. "Go outside, Molly, honey. You're breaking up."

"...Ken."

"Ken?" he repeated. "Ken who?"

"Ken Ross, who is this?"

"Chandler Landry. I'm sorry, I must have dialed too quickly."

"No, wait! I have Molly's phone. She took my car. I think she was—"

"Was what?" he demanded. "Was what?"

But the line was dead.

Chapter Eighteen

Molly parked Ken's car in the general vicinity of the curb in front of Rachel's apartment building. Ken's car was the last of her worries. Something wasn't quite right in all this.

According to the names stenciled above the rusty black mailboxes hanging just inside the entrance, Rachel's apartment was 1C. She heard the rhythmic pounding of someone's too-loud stereo and smelled the familiar, spicy scent of instant microwavable noodles wafting through the unadorned building. She smiled as she recalled that meal. It was a required staple for the college crowd.

She found 1C at the end of the hallway, to the left of and behind the stairway. Good thing it was hidden, this was her first foray into breaking and entering, and she appreciated the small measure of cover afforded by the alcove.

Bright moment number two came when she saw there was no dead bolt. Just a simple, scratched, battered knob. She dug into her purse, wondering if she had anything that might slip between the jam and the latch. Her checkbook, no. A tube of lip glass, no. Three barrettes, maybe. She held them between her teeth. A tampon, no. The tube of pepper spray she'd had for the better part of a decade, no. And her wallet. A credit card, she thought excitedly. Just like in the movies.

Only, ten minutes later she knew it was *nothing* like in the movies. She'd broken two of her credit cards, one snapped into toothlike ridges that were so sharp she sliced her knuckle in the process.

She tried a third card, but it, too, snapped. She shoved the pieces in her back pocket as she tried to think of an alternative. Not finding one, she gave the door a little kick and it popped open.

"Step one," she chided herself as she slipped inside, "check to see if the lock is sturdy."

Rachel's apartment was typical grad student. Mismatched furniture, worn cushions and a table that was covered with papers waiting to be graded and bills yet to be paid.

But nothing special. Nothing jumped out. She went into the bedroom. The double bed had neither a headboard nor a footboard, but the comforter was nice and the area tidy. Still, nothing out of place. A bed and a dresser. But something above the dresser caught her eye. Stuck in the edge of the mirror, she discovered half of a ticket stub that almost any other person on earth would have dismissed. But not Molly. The stub was for a reunion seven months earlier for the Porcellian Club. The club had been a tradition at Harvard since sometime in the late 1700s.

She got a chill.

There was only one person she knew who was a Harvard graduate *and* knew Rachel. Suddenly short of breath, she turned and discovered that very person standing in the doorway, with a gun trained in her direction.

"FIRE THAT GUY," Chandler insisted, punctuating the remark by slamming his fist against the dashboard.

"It was a dispatch screwup."

"I don't care. That deputy should never have left her alone."

"I can't fire him," Seth said, as he steered into a turn at such a high rate of speed that the SUV fishtailed briefly. "But he'll be on doughnut run until hell freezes over."

"What was he thinking?"

"Wires got crossed, Chandler. The dispatcher heard I had Jonas at the hospital and assumed that meant in custody."

"And who the hell is Ken?" Chandler growled.

"The CPA from the office next door." The dispatcher's voice came over the radio, barely audible above the peel of the sirens. "This is Landry."

"Just heard from the troupers, boss. They have Peter Geller, Jr., cuffed and en route here. Said to tell you they hit the mother load."

"What about Molly? Does he have Molly?"

Seth asked, but the reply was negative. "Patch me through to the transport vehicle."

There was some static, then another voice that said, "Womax, here."

Chandler about screamed as Seth and the trouper exchanged pleasantries. When he could stand it no more, he yelled, "Ask about Molly!"

The trouper knew nothing about Molly, and the little jerk he was carting off to jail was spewing his name, birth date, rank in the Freedom Nation—Supreme Leader—and the serial number 068.

"Have the trouper meet us someplace secluded," Chandler threatened. "I'll shove the supreme leader's supreme serial number down his supremely scrawny little throat."

"Calm down," Seth urged before he thanked the trouper. "We'll find her."

"Montana's a pretty big state," Chandler said, tasting fear as they careened into the empty parking lot.

Chandler's feet hit the pavement before Seth had brought the car to a complete stop. The door to Molly's office was open, but a quick check proved it to be empty. He dashed next door, tried the knob, found it locked and started pounding.

A milquetoast kind of guy opened the door. He seemed reluctant, scared almost, until he saw Seth appear.

"Sheriff Landry," he began, then sneezed. "I'm quite worried. Molly took my car a half hour ago and she hasn't returned."

"Where was she going?"

He shrugged his thin shoulders. "She didn't say. I only know that she was quite upset. She threatened me."

Chandler took a step closer to the little man and glared down at him. "Threatened you? How?"

"She said she would...*lick* things."

"Come again?" Seth asked.

"Lick things," Ken repeated. "I am very particular about germs and I—"

"I don't really care right this minute," Chandler cut in. "Molly is missing. What did she say to you? Did she mention anyone?"

"She used my phone and gave me hers."

Chandler looked down and recognized the phone as Molly's. He grabbed it, much to the horror of Ken, and flipped it open. "It's dead," he told Seth.

"I've got some chargers in the SUV. I'll get a list of the calls made from Ken's place."

"Can you do that without a warrant?" Ken queried.

Chandler's answer was a withering look that sent the man cowering back into his plain little office.

"See if you can get access to Molly's voice mail, too," Chandler called out.

While Seth was getting the phone records, Chandler sat sideways, half in, half out of the truck, trying different power cords on the phone until he found one that fit. He shoved the adapter into place and listened as a series of beeps and tones played. Finally he began scrolling through the menus, finally reaching the stored list of most recent calls. Jotting the numbers on the back of a fast-food napkin he'd found stuffed beneath the door handle, he quickly copied them down, then began dialing.

Because the phone stored all buttons pressed, he was able to access the same options as Molly. The first call landed him in the Human Resources Department of the college.

Since he didn't have a name, he was put on hold while they tried to find the person she'd spoken with. Chandler was only vaguely aware of Seth's activities, but he'd gathered enough bits and pieces to get that Seth was arranging for a representative to come out immediately to get them into Molly's voice mail system.

"The woman is missing and I'm on freaking hold," he grumbled. "Do you believe this?"

"Hang in there," Seth called back.

His heel nervously beat against the running board, keeping time with his speeding pulse. Just when he thought he might scream, a woman came on the line.

"May I help you?"

"You spoke to Molly Jameson a little while ago?"

"Yes."

"May I ask, about what?"

"She was interested in the employment application for one of her graduate teaching assistants."

"Rachel? Rachel Mitchell?"

"Yes, I believe so."

"Do you recall what you told her?"

"Basic information. But she was particularly interested in Miss Mitchell's mother. It had—"

Nothing helpful. He should have listened when she told him Rachel wasn't a viable suspect. If he had, she wouldn't be missing. "Thank you." Chandler disconnected and quickly dialed the second number just as a private telephone service truck pulled into the lot.

Seth dealt with the land-line issues while Chandler battled a busy signal. He went into Molly's office and found Seth. Handing over a slip of paper, he pointed to one of the numbers and said, "I can't get through on this one. Can you do a reverse and give me the name for this number?"

A guy in a dark-blue jumpsuit was working on the desk phone, pressing numbers as if playing an instrument. Seth was on his cell, speaking to yet another telephone representative, gathering information about other calls Molly might have made in the hours and minutes before she disappeared.

Seth held up his index finger, then said, "The number on her cell, the busy signal, it's to Dr. Gavin Templesman."

Chandler felt his heart sink. That wasn't any help. He knew the two of them spoke often.

"Okay," Seth began again. "From Ken's place, they've got a call to the hospital."

"Why didn't we get it?" Chandler yelled. Knowing that she had called him for help only made it worse.

"Because we didn't," Seth answered.

The fact that his brother was calm and collected helped. It was pretty much the only thing keeping him from going out of his mind.

"A call to 911," Seth announced. "Then nothing else."

"911?" Dread washed over him in strong, dizzying waves. Chandler actually felt physically ill. That had never even happened to him in combat. However, not knowing where she was or if she was all right was eating him alive. He stood helpless while his mind flashed ugly images in a taunting, cruel slide show. He couldn't stand doing nothing, so he called Shane. He'd gladly enlist every last one of his brothers in order to find Molly.

As expected, Shane went into action instantly, offering to organize a Landry posse to comb the entire county if necessary. Their only solid clue was Ken's car, so Seth put out the official word to begin a search while Chandler organized the unofficial group, who were already loading into cars and heading out.

"I can retrieve from the main system now," the nearly forgotten phone tech offered.

They gathered around the speaker phone as the messages played. Three patients asking to be rescheduled; four more needing prescription refills; a couple of hang-ups; one computerized solicitation to let her know she could have a free weekend getaway. Then they heard:

"Dr. Jameson, this is Rachel. I really need to talk to you but it has to be discreetly. Call me at home when you get this. Please, please, do not call me at the school. Thanks. I almost forgot, my home number is…"

"Play that back," Chandler demanded, listening intently as the message was repeated. "Did you hear that?"

"Yeah, something in the background," Seth agreed. "Bells?"

"Six bells," Chandler corrected. "Six bells is a ship's clock. Was Rachel in the military?"

"Give me a minute." Seth went back on his phone and rattled off the list of everyone they could think of for a search through the military records. He placed his palm over the mouthpiece and said, "This might take a few minutes."

Minutes Molly might not have. Chandler forced

his mind to go over every detail of every conversation he'd ever had with Molly. He didn't remember a single mention of anyone associated with the Navy or ships or…

"I need someone with computer skills," Chandler blurted out. "Anyone!"

Ken stepped in from the outside and raised his hand. Rolling his eyes, Chandler grabbed the up-stretched arm and practically dragged the man into the back office where he'd left his laptop.

He made quick work of connecting the machine to the phone jack and parking Ken in front of it.

"I need to know about yacht races."

"Like the America's Cup? That sort of thing??"

He nodded, recalling that Molly had used that reference once. Maybe it meant something, maybe not. He was running out of options and desperate enough to try anything. "Crew members, captains, sponsors. Whatever. Can you do that?"

Ken smiled, then sneezed all over Chandler's state-of-the-art toy. He didn't care. If Ken came up with anything, he could have the damned machine.

Shane called in to say he'd picked Taylor up and they were heading to the college. Taylor knew the campus well, so she'd be leading that search.

"Tell her thank you," Chandler asked.

He heard Taylor accept, then add, "I knew I was right about Rachel. There's no way she could have hurt—"

"Boats," Chandler interrupted. "Ask her about Rachel and boats, please."

Chandler heard a rustling noise and figured Shane was handing the phone off to Taylor. "Boats? Like in water and sails and anchors?"

"Mean anything?" he hoped.

"No. Why?"

Chandler explained about the message and added, "Do you know anyone who has anything even remotely nautical in their repertoire? Someone at the college? A professor of naval history, maybe?"

"Not my area," Taylor answered, "but I can check while we're there. Have you called Dr. Templesman?"

"Got a busy signal, why?"

"He does all the hiring for the department. He probably knows more about the lives and hobbies of the faculty."

"I'll try him back, thanks."

"Please do, Chandler. I know he'll help. He practically worships Molly. Do you have his home number?"

"I don't know."

"Let me call a friend of mine who knows his secretary, and I'll call you back with it, okay?"

"Thanks."

"Hang tough, Chandler. We'll find her."

He rubbed her face and prayed that was true. The

waiting was the worst. The only person who might know who had taken Molly wasn't talking. Chandler had half a mind to go find the Freedom Nation freak and beat him until he told or died. Either option was acceptable.

"Taylor on my phone for you!" Seth yelled.

He took two steps, then caught the phone Seth had pitched to him. "Thanks, Taylor, that was quick." He hung up and then immediately switched to his own phone to call Gavin, keeping Seth's line free for official business.

"Got something!" Ken called.

"Me, too," Seth added.

Chandler was listening to the recorded announcement and was about to start speaking when he heard the ring of bells on the tape.

"She was calling from Gavin Templesman's house," he told Seth. "Rachel was at Gavin's when she called. The same bells are on his answering machine tape."

"I found the racing rosters," Ken announced proudly, "but there must be several thousand names."

"We may not need that," Seth said, his expression cautious. "The surgeon who operated on Rachel called in. Apparently she got all worked up again. Scribbled something that they think is a mine shaft and the letter *G* over and over."

"The letter has to be for Gavin. There are mines

all over the state. We need something more specific.
We should go back to the hospital and—"

"We can't, Chandler. Rachel didn't make it."

MOLLY WALKED DELIBERATELY slowly toward the
base of the mountain, knowing that her very life
probably depended on it. He knew it, too. And
seemed to be enjoying her anguish.

"Why, Gavin?"

As he puffed out his chest, she pretended to stum-
ble, refusing to think her efforts might be futile.

"I made you, Molly. You were a pathetic little
nothing and I took you under my wing. Your parents didn't love you. I did. I made sure you finished
your education. I'm the one who helped you write
your first book. And how do you repay me?"

"I didn't know those things needed repaying."
She purposefully walked toward another bit of loose
stone, needing to repeat the process several times for
even a hope of making it out of this remote setting.
Step one was to mark the trail. She'd worry about
step two—escape—as soon as a plan came to her.
No panic—not yet!—plan!

"You left our publisher, Molly. How do you think
that made me feel? And now this."

She fell again, wincing as a bit of jagged rock
stabbed into her calf. He roughly pulled her to her
feet. "I don't know what 'this' you're referring to."

"I submitted your name for the opening as assistant department chair. I was willing to make you the first woman and the youngest ever assistant at the university. It would have been historic. Yet all I got in return was a memo from the dean saying you had declined. Declined?"

"I didn't know it mattered this much."

"I've been preparing you for this sort of opportunity for years. I've invested time, money and my expertise in you and it all seems to have been for naught."

Afraid another fall might give her away, she now had to find an alternate method. "Sorry, Gavin. You chose to be a killer and a bomber. I'm not responsible for your criminal behavior."

"I do not build bombs."

"My house blew up because it wanted to?"

"That was intended as a warning. The person who crafted the explosive made an error."

"Next you're going to tell me that you had nothing to do with the woman's torso in Spawn Creek?"

"I certainly did. I needed to set up your crisis, Molly. However, you were supposed to turn to me, not Landry. I gave you many, many opportunities to atone for your behavior, and you failed to take advantage of a single one."

"You got some poor dumb kid to murder his mother, make bombs, then kill my patient and attack Rachel all because you wanted me to take a job I've never wanted in the first place?"

His hand came up and caught her just below the eye. It happened so fast that she wasn't prepared, so when she fell, the item in her hand stabbed straight into her hand.

"That poor kid, as you call him, was a Neanderthal. Came from a long line of felons. He needed someone to bankroll him. I needed someone with bomb-making skills that I could control. We both got something out of the bargain."

"He was a patsy," she countered, pressing her fingers into her palm in an attempt to stem the flow of blood. "And what about Rachel? Is she part of this, or are you using her, too?"

"I was quite fond of Rachel and she never objected when I would inquire as to your schedule. She was a simple girl, really. So appreciative of my attentions. The way you used to be."

"She didn't die, Gavin. Guess your little patsy friend blew that one."

He smiled patiently. She'd seen that look a million times and only now saw the evil behind it.

"He didn't stab Rachel. I did. Unfortunately she recognized my map of this area and overheard me on the telephone giving directions to the warehouse the night you went on the air."

"Nice trick, by the way. How did you manage that one?"

"No trickery. A patient of mine was interviewed there. Simple deduction told me that it would again be selected as the alternate site, so it was simply a matter of threatening the safety of the entire building with too little time for them to do anything but relocate."

"The rape victim Chandler told me about? You knew about that?"

"I was there, Molly."

"Rachel was sweet and kind. She didn't deserve to be hurt. Neither did Mrs. Zarnowski."

"Sad woman," Gavin agreed. "If you recall, I referred her to you. I selected her because I knew she craved death. She thanked me when the time came."

"I'll just bet she did," Molly snorted. "Why did you need a map?"

"Peter Geller, the bomber, needed someplace to hide the weapons he was buying with the money I was paying him."

"So you drew him a map?"

"Yes. And made a copy that the police will eventually find assuming they conduct a thorough search of Rachel's apartment."

"So, you planned to frame Rachel and Peter all along?"

"Save your pity where Peter is concerned. He was a killer long before I ever entered his life. And Rachel was more a matter of serendipity. I remembered the problems you had with her brother, so when she applied for a job, I simply filed that tidbit in the back of my mind."

"So after you kill me, you expect to go back to life as usual?"

"No reason to believe otherwise."

"I think you'll be in for a rude awakening, Gavin. If anything happens to me, the Landrys will make sure you're punished."

"No delusions, Molly. It hardly seems likely that a week-long dalliance with one of them would warrant much more than a nice spray of flowers at your memorial service."

Her mind flashed a vision of her own funeral and with it came a healthy dose of terror. She reached for his arm and gave a little tug as she looked into the face of a stranger. "This isn't you, Gavin. All this over a job?"

He shoved her away, his eyes fixed and unyielding as he glared at her.

They were closing in on the hillside. She couldn't outrun a bullet, but she did have one last card to play. Now, all she had to do was remember her surgical training.

"THE KID CRACKED," Seth said when he got off the radio. "It is the Greeley mine."

"So why did Rachel have a map to the Greeley mine taped behind her bedroom mirror?" Chandler asked. "It doesn't matter. Just go faster."

He used binoculars to scan the hills ahead, looking for any sign of Molly or Gavin. For now, he wanted Molly. Once she was safe, he'd deal with the professor.

"Two o'clock!" Shane's voice crackled over the walkie talkie. "See them?"

Chandler's heart raced. "That's them!" He pointed Seth in the proper direction as four other Landry vehicles and an army of deputies raced alongside. Turning the dial, he brought Molly into focus at the same time Gavin decided to slap her to the ground.

"No!" Chandler yelled automatically. As much as it pained him to watch, he didn't dare lose sight of her.

"What?"

"Bastard hit her," he managed through tightly clenched teeth.

Seth grabbed the radio and said, "Clayton and Chance, go east. Shane, you and Sam cut west. Chandler and I are going straight ahead."

"Got it."

"On it. Chandler, you seeing this?" The question came from Sam.

Of course he was seeing it. It was hard to miss the red stain of blood on her leg and—was it—more blood on her left hand. His stomach lurched. "Yeah. I see it."

It felt like a lifetime before they were close enough so that he could forgo using the binoculars. That time did come and with it, a rush of emotion the likes of which he'd never known. Chandler braced himself as Seth brought the vehicle to a sudden stop at the edge of the tree line. They had eighty, maybe a hundred, yards to go, and he wasn't wasting another second.

Molly knew time was running out. Though it hurt like mad, she pretended to be rubbing her hand when in actuality, she was preparing her homemade weapon for attack. Assuming she could get it out of her palm.

"Hey, Gavin?" she began, stepping up her pace so that she was slightly ahead of him. "Can I ask one more question?"

"I find myself growing tired of this, Molly. I have already explained your transgressions and their resulting effect, so what more do you need to know?"

"I'm curious." She took in a deep breath and held it.

"About what."

"This," she half grunted, half screamed as she slashed at his throat with the full weight of her body.

She knew she made contact, but not if she'd been successful. All she knew was that she was on top of him, reaching and clawing for the gun still in his hand.

He kicked, she bit, legs, elbows, everything was a tangled blur. Everything but the gun hovering inches to the left of her skull.

With her injured hand, Molly was no match for him. At least she had tried. At least—

Her thought was lost in the deafening echo of the single shot.

Chapter Nineteen

Chandler slipped into the hospital room with a brightly wrapped package and a vase filled with coral-colored roses. He hoped Molly might be resting but was thrilled when those brilliant green eyes smiled a greeting the moment she saw him.

"You look much better today," he said, kissing her forehead above and below the bandage wrapped around her head.

After adding his flowers to the rapidly multiplying collection, he scooted onto the side of the bed.

"You look incredible today," she replied, winking and presenting her lips for a kiss of their own. "But then, you always look incredible."

She tasted of bittersweet chocolate. "You are very good for my ego, Molly."

"I've noticed that's a problem with you Landrys."

"You aren't supposed to care about the other Landrys. Only me."

Amusement danced in her eyes as she reached

out and ran her finger along his cheek. "All the Landrys have been very nice to me. It isn't fair to ask me to pick a favorite."

"Actually—" he paused to press his lips against the palm of her hand "—family rules state that you must declare your favorite." He placed the box in her lap. "Besides, I brought you a nice present."

"You brought me a nice present yesterday."

"That was a robe. You needed that, so it doesn't really count as an *official* present."

"And the day before that."

He stroked his chin, pretending to forget about the basket of tropical fruit he'd overnighted from Hawaii. "Food. Perishable. Doesn't count, either."

When she reached for the bow, he placed his hands on hers. "Did you hear the news?"

He saw a flicker of pain pass across her face, and he wished more than anything he could make it go away. "Gavin's autopsy? Yes. Chance came and told me. He was afraid I'd hear it through the hospital gossip mill."

"Pretty weird, though, huh?"

She nodded. "But the tumor explains a great deal. Practically everything. Gavin was very nice to me once, and I think I'd like to remember him like that."

"It's still weird."

"A right-frontal-lobe tumor can cause the loss of ability to control urges and the failure to anticipate and appreciate consequences."

He moved to give her a long, deep, lingering kiss. "I get really hot when you talk doctor to me."

"You get hot if I scratch my nose."

"That hurts, Molly," he teased, clutching his heart. "It's completely true, but it hurts all the same. Open your present."

She tore into the fancy pink paper, shredding it until the box was revealed. A little laugh gurgled in her throat when she saw the day's reward. "A new cell phone. Thank you, Chandler."

"It comes with a new wall, too," he joked.

"I heard you went a little nuts in my office."

"A little."

Her expression stilled and grew more serious. "I can't believe everything you did to try to find me."

"See, there are times when a large family is a plus."

"I'm a changed woman in that respect," she swore. "I will never doubt the wisdom of having so many strapping Landry men in my life."

"Really?"

Oops, she thought, *I've crossed that imaginary line. Time to backpedal.* "Don't look so panicked, Chandler. It was a figure of speech."

"Open the box."

"Why?"

"This phone has some special features, and I want to make sure you can use them."

She felt an awkward tension in the air. Nothing

she could define, but something was off. "I'm very capable, Chandler. I can read the manual. I'm going to be here another week, thanks to you."

"We don't know that it *was* me."

"Face it, Chandler, you shot me in the head."

"You were grazed," he groaned. "And we all had guns up there."

"Except me," she joked, waving her bandaged hand. "I had to rely on my wit and cunning."

Though his eyes rolled, she saw the smile tugging at the corners of his mouth. "Kudos for creativity, honey, but what made you think you could make a shiv out of a credit card?"

"It was all I had," she reminded him. "I wasn't about to do *nothing*."

"I'm glad," he said, his voice smooth and inviting. "You don't know what it was like watching you through the binoculars, knowing I might not make it in time."

She felt his involuntary shiver and it touched her. "I'm glad you came, and I'm glad you brought the cavalry."

"Thank you."

"I'm not real thrilled that you shot me in the head."

"Molly!"

"Sorry," she said, swallowing her laughter. "I just like to see the way you get all frazzled and blustery when I say that."

"Little-old ladies get frazzled. Men get pissed."

"Sorry, I wasn't challenging your testosterone level."

"Finish opening your gift," he urged.

After removing mounds of protective wrapping, she finally pulled the phone from the box. "Very nice. It takes pictures, too! Thank you."

Chandler took the phone and pressed buttons as he spoke. "This one turns it on."

"I never would have thought to use the power button."

He slipped off the bed, kneeling closer to her so they both had the same angle, "Sarcasm is not appreciated. Pay attention."

"I am." Though it was difficult to keep her mind focused when he was close enough for her to smell his cologne. His breath tickled the small hairs on her arm as he continued to press buttons. She sensed him growing more frustrated. "I really can read the manual."

"Hush." He worked some more, then smiled. "Push the down arrow."

"Okay."

She did, and a very silly photograph of Clayton appeared on the small screen. He was holding a sign with her name on it. "'Molly.' Very creative."

"Push it again."

She did. Her heart skipped. It was a picture of Chance this time. His sign read, Will.

"Again."

There was a slight tremor in her finger as she scrolled to the next one of Sam. His sign read, You.

Shane appeared, holding the word Please.

It could be, "Molly, will you please get well soon?" Or "Molly, will you please forgive me for shooting you?" Do not get your hopes up.

But she couldn't help herself. She sucked in a breath and hit the key. Seth appeared, and the word Marry was crystal clear.

"And again."

Her eyes welled up with tears when Chandler's image appeared. He was down on one knee, holding a small jewelry box in one hand, and the word Me in the other. *Oh, man. This is so sweet! I love him.*

"If you do it really, really fast, we look like a homemade comic strip."

She laughed through her tears. "This was a very elaborate proposal."

"It's not over yet." He reached into his pocket and pulled out the box from the photograph. Slowly he eased open the top to reveal the most beautiful ring she'd ever seen. A large emerald surrounded by diamonds, set in platinum.

He cleared his throat, looked deeply into her eyes and asked, "Molly, will you please marry me?"

"I...I," she couldn't believe it.

"Wait a second." He scrambled up off the floor and went to the window.

"Don't you dare throw that ring out the window! Give me a minute to think first."

He turned and laughed. "I'm not throwing the ring away. I just realized I forgot a pretty big part of this." He tossed back the drapes and she gasped.

The five other brothers were standing on a raised platform outside her window. Stretched between them was yet another sign.

He didn't read the words to her. Instead Chandler turned, his head slightly tilted, and flashed a brilliant smile. "I love you."

"I love you, too."

Chandler came over and kissed her lips as he slipped the ring on her finger.

It was the most incredible, most wonderful proposal in the world. Made even better when, on cue, the outside Landrys, sporting bullhorns, started chanting in unison.

"We want Molly. We want Molly."

* * * * *

Turn the page for a sneak peek of
Kelsey Roberts's next

LANDRY BROTHERS *book,*
CHARMED AND DANGEROUS,

available this December
from Harlequin Intrigue.

Chapter One

"I don't need a baby-sitter, due respect, sir. I am fully capable of taking care of myself." J. J. Barnes was not happy, and she made sure her narrowed glare indicated that point. The barely healed scar on her side itched and pulled. Maybe tomorrow she could compartmentalize and put the incident behind her once and for all.

FBI Associate Director Terrance "Red" Andrews didn't seem impressed by her rhetoric. In fact, his white brows arched a caution in response to her tone.

J.J. immediately adjusted her attitude. Outwardly, at least. Inside, her stomach churned as waves of queasiness rocked through her. She covered by leaning forward to grip the back of the burgundy leather chair as if to argue the point.

"You've been released back to full duty, Agent Barnes. But that doesn't solve the immediate problem." He peered up at her above the rims of his half glasses, his blue eyes stern and unyielding. "I would assume that after that debacle with the Visnopov matter, you'd be more…circumspect."

"I am, sir," she assured him. "Two weeks in the hospital and a month recuperating at home gave me plenty of time to analyze and review my actions. I realize now that I should have arranged for a follow team prior to the meeting."

"It wasn't a *meeting,* Agent Barnes. It was a beat down. The government has invested a great deal of time and money in this investigation. We'd like you to stay alive until the U.S. attorney gets in front of a grand jury. Understood?"

"Yes, sir."

Andrews shuffled papers around on his cluttered desk until he found a thin folder and held it out to her. "You *will* accept a protective detail."

"But, sir—"

He lifted a finger, silencing her immediately. He smiled, the expression falling somewhere between grudging respect and utter exasperation. "Sit, Barnes."

She readily followed the order. She was still sore from the surgery and the fatigue that just refused to go away no matter how many hours she slept. She didn't know much about having a spleen removed, but she guessed the lingering maladies were side effects. Hopefully, they'd go away soon. J.J. prided herself on her fitness. She was the reigning female record holder on the obstacle course, and now she was having trouble making it through the day without a nap.

She took the folder, but she didn't open it immediately. It was accepted practice to wait for a superior's go-ahead before diving into anything. If she'd followed that procedure, maybe Visnopov's goons wouldn't have—"

"I know you, Barnes," he said, raking his stubby fingers through his thick shock of white hair. "I knew you'd balk at the idea of protection, so I came up with an incentive for you."

Her mood brightened slightly. "Sir?"

Nodding, he pointed at the folder. "We've lost three of the critical Visnopov witnesses so far," he began as she perused color photos of the victims. "You were almost the fourth."

J.J. wasn't sure how to react. She could have argued that it wasn't totally her fault. Her cover was blown the minute the first member of Visnopov's crew was arrested. It would have been nice if the U.S. attorney had coordinated the arrest. Given her a heads up. But arguing—in Andrews's eyes—conveyed a complete lack of personal responsibility, and she wasn't about to give him any more reasons to question her abilities.

"The Visnopovs are going to come after you again."

A frisson of dread slid down her spine. She straightened her back and kept her gaze steady with effort. "I assumed as much."

"The Marshal's Service will handle the particulars."

A groan escaped her lips before she could prevent it. J.J. hoped he hadn't noticed it as she turned to the next page. Her interest was instantly piqued. This wasn't a picture of a criminal or a victim. This was an official head shot of a U.S. marshal. Turning to the back of the photograph, she read the particulars. Denise Howard, 51, 25 years with the service. "These people are my protective detail?"

"No," Andrews said as she continued to examine the file.

Martin Newell, 49. Lynn Selznick, 31. She looked more like a college coed than a Federal agent. Then she saw the last picture and her heart skipped. Cody Landry was as handsome as she remembered. "But?" She glanced up at Andrews and said, "I don't follow, sir. These people are—"

"Suspects in the murder of Alex Maslonovic," Andrews explained. "We have every reason to believe that someone inside the U.S. Marshal's Service is a mole. Your assignment is to find out which one is responsible."

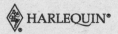

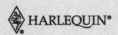

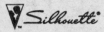

From first love to forever, these love stories are fairy tale romances for today's woman.

Modern, passionate reads that are powerful and provocative.

♥ Silhouette
SPECIAL EDITION™

Emotional, compelling stories that capture the intensity of living, loving and creating a family in today's world.

♥ Silhouette
INTIMATE MOMENTS™

A roller-coaster read that delivers romantic thrills in a world of suspense, adventure and more.

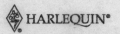
HARLEQUIN®

INTRIGUE

**Don't miss the latest book in
Mallory Kane's Ultimate Agents series,
coming in August 2005.**

SEEKING ASYLUM

To thwart deadly experiments, FBI agent Eric Baldwyn had
to go undercover to infiltrate a private mental facility.
Only Dr. Rachel Harper knew his true identity, and she
agreed to help him uncover the secrets going on behind
locked doors. And while danger lurked, the burgeoning
chemistry between them made Eric wonder if they
could seek asylum in each other's arms.

Available at your favorite retail outlet.

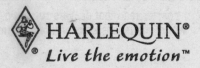